"Will you marry me, darlin'?"

"*Marry* you? Are you mad?"

"I may be. Something strange is going on. There's magic between us. Don't you feel it? If you won't marry me, will you at least come home to Texas with me?"

"You *are* mad. I'm not going anywhere with you."

"Why not?"

"You're practically a stranger. I don't know anything about you."

"We can soon remedy that."

He started to kiss her again, but she averted her mouth. "Don't do that," she protested.

"I thought you liked it."

"You were mistaken."

"Was I?"

She'd often heard the term "rakish grin," but she'd never completely understood the power of one until that moment. When he looked at her and grinned in that captivating way, she melted. This tall Texan was totally beyond her experience; he was *way* out of her league.

But she kissed him again anyhow....

Dear Reader,

The joys of summer are upon us—along with some July fireworks from Silhouette Desire!

The always wonderful Jennifer Greene presents our July MAN OF THE MONTH in *Prince Charming's Child*. A contemporary romance version of *Sleeping Beauty*, this title also launches the author's new miniseries, HAPPILY EVER AFTER, inspired by those magical fairy tales we loved in childhood. And ever-talented Anne Marie Winston is back with a highly emotional reunion romance in *Lovers' Reunion*. The popular miniseries TEXAS BRIDES by Peggy Moreland continues with the provocative story of *That McCloud Woman*. Sheiks abound in Judith McWilliams's *The Sheik's Secret*, while a plain Jane is wooed by a millionaire in Jan Hudson's *Plain Jane's Texan*. And Barbara McCauley's new dramatic miniseries, SECRETS!, debuts this month with *Blackhawk's Sweet Revenge*.

We've got more excitement for you next month—watch for the premiere of the compelling new Desire miniseries THE TEXAS CATTLEMAN'S CLUB. Some of the sexiest, most powerful men in the Lone Star State are members of this prestigious club, and they all find love when they least expect it! You'll learn more about THE TEXAS CATTLEMAN'S CLUB in our August Dear Reader letter, along with an update on Silhouette's new continuity, THE FORTUNES OF TEXAS, debuting next month.

And this month, join in the celebrations by treating yourself to all six passionate Silhouette Desire titles.

Enjoy!

Joan Marlow Golan
Senior Editor, Silhouette Desire

Please address questions and book requests to:
Silhouette Reader Service
U.S.: 3010 Walden Ave., P.O. Box 1325, Buffalo, NY 14269
Canadian: P.O. Box 609, Fort Erie, Ont. L2A 5X3

PLAIN JANE'S TEXAN

JAN HUDSON

SILHOUETTE *Desire*

Published by Silhouette Books

America's Publisher of Contemporary Romance

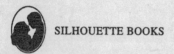

SILHOUETTE BOOKS

ISBN 0-373-76229-1

PLAIN JANE'S TEXAN

Copyright © 1999 by Janece O. Hudson

All rights reserved. Except for use in any review, the reproduction
or utilization of this work in whole or in part in any form by any
electronic, mechanical or other means, now known or hereafter
invented, including xerography, photocopying and recording, or in
any information storage or retrieval system, is forbidden without
the written permission of the editorial office, Silhouette Books,
300 East 42nd Street, New York, NY 10017 U.S.A.

All characters in this book have no existence outside the imagination of
the author and have no relation whatsoever to anyone bearing the same
name or names. They are not even distantly inspired by any individual
known or unknown to the author, and all incidents are pure invention.

This edition published by arrangement with Harlequin Books S.A.

® and TM are trademarks of Harlequin Books S.A., used under license.
Trademarks indicated with ® are registered in the United States Patent
and Trademark Office, the Canadian Trade Marks Office and in other
countries.

Visit us at www.romance.net

Printed in U.S.A.

JAN HUDSON,

a winner of the Romance Writers of America RITA Award, is a native Texan who lives with her husband in historically rich Nacogdoches, the oldest town in Texas. Formerly a licensed psychologist, she taught college psychology for over a decade before becoming a full-time author. Jan loves to write fast-paced stories laced with humor, fantasy and adventure, and with bold characters who reach beyond the mundane and celebrate life.

For my special aunts,
Barbara and Benye, and in loving memory
of Mamie, Louise and Estelle

One

As Matt Crow stood at the altar of a small Episcopal church in Akron, Ohio, gussied up in a tuxedo and his dress boots, he saw an angel, an honest-to-God angel. He hadn't seen anything so beautiful since he'd left Texas at dawn. He couldn't take his eyes off her.

Matt forgot about the crowd gathered for the wedding. The music preceding the bride's entry became a faint melody somewhere in the back of his mind. His total attention was on the angel coming toward him.

Instead of a diaphanous white robe, she wore a wine-colored gown, and he didn't see wings sprouting from her back, but otherwise she was absolutely celestial. Sunlight shining through the stained glass window shimmered around her head like a halo and turned her hair to strands of spun silver and pale gold interlaced with pearls.

Spellbound, he watched as she slowly approached the altar, her gaze lowered, her hands clutching a large bouquet of lilies and roses. Only when she took her place beside the others gathered there did she lift her chin. Her long lashes swept upward to reveal the most gorgeous eyes he'd ever seen in his life.

An angel's eyes.

So pale and haunting a blue that against her golden skin they seemed like liquid sky. His mouth went dry. The world stopped.

Totally terrified, Eve Ellison clutched her bouquet as if the flowers were a lifeline in the turbulent sea of emotions threatening to engulf her. Why had she ever agreed to be the maid of honor? She'd tried to talk Irish out of it, tried to convince her sister that one of her poised and glamorous friends would be much better, but Irish wouldn't hear of it.

"Eve, don't be a goose," Irish had said. "I wouldn't dream of having anyone but my little sister for my maid of honor."

Eve had peered over her glasses and scowled. "I am not by any stretch of the imagination your *little* sister. I'm damned near six feet tall and not the type for ruffles and sweetheart necklines. I'll do the flowers, I'll bake the cake, I'll even make cutesy little bags of birdseed and potpourri for the guests to toss, but please don't ask me to put on a Scarlett O'Hara dress and walk down that aisle in front of everybody. Irish, you're the beauty of the family, you're the model who loves the limelight, not me. I'd feel like a fool.''

But Irish had planted her fists on her hips and gotten that determined look on her face, the one that said she planned on getting her way, no matter what. ''Eve Ellison, I don't know where you get your dumb ideas. You'll be a lovely maid of honor. You're much more beautiful than I ever was.''

Eve had snorted. ''Yeah, sure. Everyone's talking about how I have to beat off the hordes of men with a baseball bat. Sis, I haven't even had a date in almost a year.''

''Then the men in Cleveland are blind. Anyone can see that you're lovely. I suspect that it's your attitude rather than your looks keeping them away. And…well, you could do a little something with your hair.''

Her hand had automatically gone to her head. ''What's wrong with my hair?''

''Other than the fact that it looks as if it were last cut with a weed whacker, hasn't been brushed thoroughly in a week, and is tied into a lopsided mess with a shoe string?''

Eve had jutted her jaw. ''Yeah, other than that?''

Irish had burst into laughter. ''I swear, Eve, I think you go out of your way to look grungy. No makeup, shapeless clothes. What are you trying to prove?''

Actually Eve wasn't trying to prove anything. She simply didn't think much about her appearance. Never had. Irish had always been the beauty; Eve had the brains. Not that Irish was dumb, of course. She wasn't. Irish was very bright, but she'd always been more interested in clothes and makeup and drama. Eve had been content to hide away with a book or her paints or a stray cat. She'd always cared more for digging in the dirt among the flowers and vegetables than polishing her fingernails.

Predictably, Irish had decided that the time had come for Eve to pay some attention to her appearance, and nothing would do but for the two of them to spend a week in New York. The prospective groom, Dr. Kyle Rutledge, agreed that it was a splendid idea and insisted on bankrolling the excursion.

Now here Eve was, her hair styled, her nails polished, her face made up, wearing new contact lenses and a Scarlett O'Hara gown and feeling like a damned fool. Sure that everyone must be staring at her, she'd kept her eyes on the toes of her satin pumps as she walked down the aisle to the altar, praying earnestly that she wouldn't throw up or keel over. Terrified as she was, the walk had seemed ten miles long.

The first thing she saw when she finally looked up was a pair of flashing black eyes staring at her. The man, who she assumed was Kyle's cousin, wasn't just staring, he was gaping. He probably thought she looked like a damned fool, too. She wanted to disappear in a puff of smoke.

Automatically, she began to draw in her shoulders to protect her heart, but the new bra Irish had insisted she buy was taut as a bow string. The blasted thing gouged and pinched her and prevented her familiar postural shield.

So instead of drawing in like a turtle, she lifted her chin and defiantly gaped back.

Gaping at him wasn't difficult. The man was gorgeous. Six and a half feet of gorgeous. Thick dark hair, cleft chin, sexy mouth, shoulders a yard wide.

He winked at her, and she almost pitched over on her nose. Heat rose from her chest and spread over her throat. Before she made a complete idiot of herself, she turned quickly as the congregation rose and Irish and their dad started down the aisle.

This must be Matt Crow, Eve thought as the wedding march swelled. She'd met Kyle's cousin, Jackson Crow, at the rehearsal and subsequent dinner the night before, but Jackson's brother couldn't make it to Ohio until that morning, and Kyle's brother Smith hadn't been able to make the wedding at all. Even so, never had Eve seen so many tall, handsome men as the bunch of Texans Irish had met on her jaunt to find a millionaire. Eve had thought that Jackson was particularly good-looking, but his younger brother was unbelievable. He took her breath away.

Little colored dots began to dance in front of her eyes. Eve shook herself, sucked in a deep breath, and turned to face the priest.

Matt couldn't keep his eyes or his thoughts off the maid of honor. She must be Irish's younger sister. Ann? Karen? Lisa? For the life of him, he couldn't remember. When Irish or Kyle had mentioned her, her name hadn't registered. Everything about her registered now.

When Kyle finally kissed his bride and turned to grin like a possum at the audience, Matt could hardly wait until the bridal party got outside and he could make the angel's acquaintance. Moments later the best man, Flint Durham, lucky dog, offered his arm to her, and they followed Kyle and Irish up the aisle. Jackson and one of the bridesmaids went next. Matt crooked his arm for Kim Devlin, another bridesmaid, and they brought up the rear.

"What's Irish's sister's name?" he asked Kim as they hurried from the church.

Kim grinned. "Eve. Beautiful, isn't she?"

"You got that right."

Matt tried to make his way to Eve, but the group was herded by a photographer into an area for picture taking, and there was no opportunity to speak with her. Matt prayed that Jackson didn't set his sights on Eve, and for once he was lucky. His big brother was busy trying to hustle another of the bridesmaids—a dark sultry type named Olivia.

Jackson, the prime stud of Texas who usually had willing women lined up four deep, put his arm around the woman's waist and whispered in her ear. Olivia looked at him as if he were something she'd stepped in on a walk through the cow pasture and said, "I've told you for the last time, I'm not interested in anything you have to offer. And if you don't move your hand, I'll break your fingers."

Matt nearly broke up laughing, and when the photographer said, "Smile!," he didn't have to put on.

Matt was tempted to carry Jackson high for striking out for once in his life. Jackson never struck out. He was the luckiest son-of-a-gun in the world, and everything had always come easy for him. All his life, Matt had to bust his butt for the breaks. But he wasn't in the mood to razz his brother; he was preoccupied with meeting Eve. He could only stand and stare at her as she posed with Irish and their family for more pictures.

She had totally captivated him, and Matt couldn't exactly define what it was that enthralled him so. Sure, she was beautiful, but he'd seen his share of beautiful women. Something else about her struck a chord deep within him. There was a guilelessness about her, sort of an innocence that shone in her pale eyes and made him want to protect her. And possess her.

Matt knew as sure as shootin' that this was the woman for him. Knew it as certainly as if it had been announced with a blare of trumpets and a voice from the clouds.

As he watched, frown lines marred her smooth forehead. He had the craziest urge to hop on a horse, ride through the crowd, pull her up in the saddle with him, and rescue her from whatever was making her unhappy.

Eve would sooner have had her fingernails pulled out with pliers than pose for pictures—especially beside Irish. Irish was so astonishingly beautiful, and she herself was so...not. Since she was a kid in grammar school, people had always looked at her with amazement and said, "*You're* Irish Ellison's sister?"

Many nights she had cried herself to sleep after such hurtful comments or after being teased by her classmates for her beanpole gawkiness and her over-bite.

Eve had learned soon enough that she had to settle for brains because her sister got all the beauty from the barrel before she arrived. And after Irish became a model with her face on magazine covers, things had gotten worse for Eve, who was in high school with braces, zits, no boobs, knobby knees and a head above most of the boys on the basketball team—though at least the braces had remedied the overbite.

She tried to inch away after the family picture, but Irish grabbed her arm. "Oh, no, you don't. I want another of just you and me."

"Good Lord, why? I might break the camera."

Irish laughed. "You goose. You're gorgeous."

"You need glasses."

"Matt Crow thinks you're gorgeous, too," Irish whispered as she arranged her skirt. "He hasn't taken his eyes off you. I definitely think he's interested."

"Him? In *me*? Get real, Sis. I'm not his type. And don't you dare do any matchmaking. I'll put a spell on you, and you'll grow hairy warts on your nose on your honeymoon."

Irish only laughed.

Before Matt had a chance to talk to Eve, everybody was whisked into limos and taken to a hotel. As soon as they arrived, he strode toward the reception area, his eyes scanning the crowd.

When he finally spotted Eve across the room talking to his grandfather, Cherokee Pete, Matt tried to make his way toward the blond beauty, but his mother stopped him with a firm grip on his wrist and insisted that he meet Irish's parents.

"I swear you look pretty as a picture," Kyle's grandfather said, a broad smile splitting his weathered, wrinkled face. "Puts me in mind of an angel."

Eve laughed. The old fellow, who was well into his eighties, was every bit as charming as his grandsons. Close to six feet tall, he stood ramrod straight. With his dark eyes and high cheekbones, a gift of his Native American ancestry, he was still an imposing presence. "Thank you, Mr. Beamon. You look very handsome in your tuxedo." And despite the long braids trailing over his shoulders, he honestly did.

He let out a bark of laughter. "Like a damned fool is what you mean. Never worn one of these gawldurn getups in my life, but I didn't want to come in my overalls and embarrass your sister. I'm right fond of Irish, you know. And even if I am decked out in my bib and tucker, I'll have none of this 'Mr. Beamon' stuff. Everybody calls me Cherokee Pete or just plain Pete."

"Then just plain Pete it is. And I'll let you in on a little secret. I'd rather be in overalls or blue jeans myself. Irish has told me so much about you and your trading post in Texas that I'd love to see it. Do you really sculpt animals from logs with a chain saw the same way Kyle does?"

"Yep. Taught Kyle everything he knows. He was the only one of my grandsons who took after it, but I reckon he won't be doing much log sculptin' now that he's going back to doctorin'. I've got four grandsons, you know. Kyle's the first one to get married. Got three left. Kyle's brother, Smith, who's got himself stove up from a wreck right now, and Jackson and Matt. They're not bad-looking boys." He cocked his head, and a twinkle came into his eyes. "Any way I could interest you in one?"

Eve grinned. "I don't think so."

"You sure? I'd be willin' to throw in a couple of million, and you could take your pick. 'Course Jackson's the oldest, and I'd like to see him making a family pretty soon. Them boys is past time to be settling down."

Despite his appearance, his folksy talk and his lifestyle, she knew that the wily old man could make good on his offer. He'd struck oil on his property many years before and was loaded. "Do they know that you're trying to sell them?"

He winked at her. "Oh, that would be just between you and me. I've about got your daddy talked into retiring and moving down to Texas with your mother. Like I told Al and Beverly, we've got a big spread down there. Lots of room. Why don't you come on down with them?"

"I would love a place with more room for all my animals, but my job is in Cleveland."

"You got animals?"

"Lots of them. My mother swears that I can't resist a stray. They seem to always find their way to my door. I have two cats, Charlie Chan and Pansy, a goat named Elmer, a pig, a rooster, two ducks, four dogs and—"

"Could I interest you two in some champagne?" a deep voice said behind her.

Eve turned to find Matt Crow holding three stemmed glasses, two cupped between the long fingers of his left hand, another in his right. He held the one out to her and smiled.

She glanced upward, looked into his face, and tried to say something intelligent. No words came. Not a croak. Not a whisper. Not a stammer. Nothing.

He lifted his brows and offered the glass again. She took the champagne and clutched the flute in a death grip.

"Grandpa Pete?"

"I wouldn't mind one of those to wet my whistle," Pete said, taking one of the remaining two.

"Did I interrupt something?" Matt asked.

"I was just trying to convince Eve to move to Texas so she could have lots of room for her animals. Eve, this here's my grandson, Matt."

Matt's dark eyes bore into hers. "Oh, do you have animals?"

She tried again to speak, but her mouth was dry. She took a sip of champagne and managed to whisper, "Yes."

"Did he convince you?" Matt asked.

Convince her? Of what? She tried to think, to recall the earlier conversation, but thinking was like trying to walk in knee-deep mud. He obviously noticed her perplexity because he smiled and said, "Did Grandpa Pete convince you to move to Texas? Sounds like a great idea to me."

She shook her head. "Impossible."

"Nothing is impossible." He tossed back his wine in one swallow and set the glass aside. "Dance?"

"I—I'm not much of a dancer."

"I don't believe it. Angels float on air." He peeled her fingers from the stemmed glass and handed it to Pete. "Come," he said, holding out his arms to her.

She stepped into his arms as if it were the most

natural thing in the world, and they began to waltz. Eve, who'd always had two left feet, glided across the floor in perfect synchronization with Matt's lead.

They danced on and on, swirling around the floor until laughter rippled from her throat like bubbles from Dom Perignon. He smiled down at her, his eyes shining like a starry midnight, and an unbelievable thrill went through her body.

The tempo of the music changed to a ballad, and he pulled her close. Her forehead rested perfectly in the hollow of his cheek. Still in perfect sync, their steps became slow, but as their bodies touched, her pulse began to accelerate. She could feel heat radiate from him, and his warm scent, a unique mixture of spice, citrus and musk, filled her nostrils and titillated the synapses of her spine. Everything emanating from Matt Crow proclaimed his total, visceral maleness, and everything in her responded. Chill bumps raced across her skin while a writhing hot mass swelled deep within.

Eve began to tremble.

She pushed away. "I—I don't want this."

The expression in his eyes almost made her weep. "What don't you want?"

"This. This—" She pushed against his chest, but his arms held her fast, and their feet still moved in cadence. Her reaction to Matt Crow was scary, and she was quickly getting in over her head. He was way out of her league.

"Explain."

Feeling as awkward as a teenager with a crush on a movie star, she shook her head. She was too embarrassed to explain her feelings. After all, she was simple, gawky Eve Ellison, and he was...well, he was a sophisticated man, a Texas millionaire used to bevies of beautiful, sophisticated women.

He pulled her back against him, and his lips brushed her ear. "It seems almost overwhelming, doesn't it? From the moment I saw you, I felt as if I'd been kicked by a bull. I knew that you were the most perfect woman God had ever created. It's only right that you should be named Eve." His tongue traced the curve of her ear. "Offer me an apple, sugar, and I'm yours body and soul."

Eve's knees gave. She sagged against him.

"Let's find someplace private," Matt whispered. "I think I may die if I don't kiss you."

She thought that she might die, too. He was a smooth one, all right. Oh, she knew his type. She knew that he was feeding her a line a mile long, but her brain didn't seem to have one iota of control over her body. Despite her every effort, her head nodded.

With his arm around her waist, he guided her from the dance floor and maneuvered her through the crowd. Her pulse was racing, her heart pounding, and she felt in imminent danger of hyperventilating. She should dig in her heels and put a stop to this nonsense right now. But her feet didn't pay any attention, either. They padded right along beside Matt like a lamb to slaughter.

He located a secluded alcove and pulled her into it. Instantly his mouth covered hers. She almost fainted. Her hormones began to run amok like crazed, marauding elephants smashing into each other and flattening everything in their path. She plastered herself against him and kissed him back.

After about five minutes of fervent French kissing, Matt pulled away. His breathing was ragged. "Good God in Heaven, darlin'. I think I'm having a heart attack. Will you marry me?"

Some measure of sanity returned to Eve's brain. "*Marry* you? Certainly not. Are you mad?"

"I may be. Something strange is going on, that's for sure. There's magic between us. Don't you feel it? If you won't marry me, will you at least come home to Texas with me? If we live together for a while, maybe you could get used to the idea."

The marauding elephants stopped dead in their tracks. "You *are* mad. I'm not going anywhere with you."

"Why not?"

"I should think it would be obvious. You're practically a stranger. I don't know anything about you."

"We can soon remedy that. What do you want to know?"

He started to kiss her again, but she averted her mouth. "Don't do that," she protested.

"I thought you liked it."

"You were mistaken."

"Was I?"

She'd often heard the term "rakish grin," but she'd never completely understood the power of one until that moment. When he looked at her and grinned in that captivating way, she melted. This tall Texan was totally beyond her experience; he was way, way, *way* out of her league, but she kissed him again anyhow.

A strident noise blared between them, and she startled. He cursed. "Damned phone. Sorry, honey. It must be an emergency.'' Scowling, he pulled a slim cellular unit from inside his coat. "This had better be good,'' he said to the caller. After a minute of listening, he added a few other colorful phrases. "I'm on my way.'' He stuck the phone back into his pocket and took her into his arms once more. "I have to leave. Come home with me,'' he murmured as he nipped her ear and nuzzled her neck.

"Impossible. I can't just run off on a whim. I have a career. I have obligations.''

"Quit your job. You won't need to work. I'll take care of you. Come with me, Eve.''

"Take *care* of—'' A bucket of cold reality splashed her, and she stiffened in his arms. What kind of person did he think she was? "No way.''

Matt cupped her nape and searched her face. "Why not? Kim said that you weren't married or engaged. Is there someone else?''

Deciding to take the easy way out, Eve crossed her fingers behind her back in a childish gesture. "Yes. Yes there is. Charlie.''

"Ditch him. You couldn't care much about the guy and kiss me the way you did.''

"You're wrong. I adore Charlie. We've lived together for the last two years. I couldn't leave him.'' At least that part was true.

Standing with his gaze downcast, Matt was quiet for a long time. Then he looked up. "I see.'' If Eve hadn't known better, she would have thought there were tears in his eyes. A trick of the lighting, she was sure. "For a while there, I really thought this was it.'' He gently kissed her forehead. "Charlie is a lucky man. So long, angel. Would you tell everyone goodbye for me? I've got an emergency, and it's something serious. I've gotta go.''

Not trusting herself to speak, she nodded, then he was gone. It was a good thing she hadn't fallen for his slick line. And it was simply a line, she reminded herself. Matt Crow moved in another world, one far removed from her simple life. Irish, the gorgeous, super-cool ex-New York model, could handle this kind of stuff, but Eve? No way. A guy like Matt would have only broken her heart.

Two

Holding the mail between her teeth and juggling a ripping sack of groceries, twenty pounds of cat litter, her shoulder bag and a bulging briefcase, Eve kicked the front door closed just as the phone began to ring.

The sack ripped another few inches. She dropped the litter and her briefcase and tried to grab the sack to save the eggs.

Too late. The blasted thing split completely, and she only managed to mash a loaf of bread and a half gallon of Rocky Road against her body. The egg carton landed with an ominous splat beside the mushrooms; oranges and onions and cans went rolling every which way.

The phone continued to ring.

Eve made an exasperated noise, marched to the phone and snatched it up. "Heh-woe."

"Eve?" a man's voice said. "Eve Ellison?"

She spat out the letters she still clutched between her teeth. "Sorry. Yes, this is Eve Ellison, and I don't want any insurance protection for my credit cards, cemetery plots or—"

"Eve, this is Matt Crow."

She dropped the mangled bread and ice cream carton on the table and sank into a chair. "Matt Crow?"

He chuckled. "Yes, we met at the wedding last weekend. Surely you haven't forgotten me so soon."

Forgotten him? Fat chance. Hadn't the memories of him nearly driven her up the wall for the past few days? "No, I remember you," she said, fighting a tremor in her voice and trying to be casual. "You'll have to forgive me, it's been one of those days—no, make that one of those weeks, and it's only Wednesday."

"I've had a few of those lately myself. Problems?"

"Lots."

"Want to tell me about them?"

Something about the gentle tone of his voice made her want to pour out everything to him. Instead, she said, "I'm sure that you don't want to hear my sad story."

"You're wrong, Eve. What's happened?"

"You name it." She tried to laugh, but the sound seem strangled. "I had a blowout and took out two garbage cans and a fire hydrant before I could stop the car. I received a notice yesterday from the Dog Warden of the City of Cleveland Kennel that I'm in violation of a city ordinance, and I have to get rid of some of my animals or risk having them seized. I figure that's partly because of Elmer and Minerva getting out last week, and Elmer eating Mrs. Gaither's sweetpeas or it might have been Mrs. Ramsey who complained about—''

"Whoa!" Matt said, chuckling. "Who are Elmer and Minerva?"

"Sorry, I'm ranting. Elmer is a goat and Minerva is a pig."

"A goat and a pig in the city?"

Eve sighed. "I've been trying to find them homes. Would you like a goat?"

"I live in a high-rise, but I could talk to Grandpa Pete about it."

"Thanks, but Elmer isn't the only problem. The logical solution is to move to another house."

"You could always move to Texas," he said, his tone conjuring up visions of hot nights on cool sheets. "My offer is still open."

Her heart stumbled. Her face flushed. He was obviously teasing her again, but she didn't know how to handle such comments. She didn't want to make a serious response and have him think that she was so unsophisticated, but she wasn't experienced in social banter with men like him.

"Eve?"

Forcing gaiety, she laughed and said, "I was just trying to picture Elmer and Minerva and the others in your living room. I'm afraid I'll have to pass, but after meeting Godzilla today, I might be tempted."

"Godzilla?"

"My new boss. They brought him in as the creative director, but the last creative thought he had was in 1989. Only thing he had going for him was that he worked in a *New York* agency. That job should have been mine, darn it. Sorry, I didn't mean to whine, and I've been babbling on and on.''

"You weren't whining or babbling, and I enjoy talking to you. We didn't get to spend enough time together at the wedding, and I've been putting out fires ever since I left. Say, I'm going to be in Cleveland in a day or two, and now that we're practically family, I was hoping that we might get together for dinner...or something.''

A rush of panic swept over Eve. Even though he made her knees weak and her heart go pitter-patter, she felt completely out of her element with a man like Matt. Being around him too much might make her have goofy ideas—like believing they weren't totally mismatched. She knew that he was simply making a duty call since he was going to be in Cleveland and since they were "practically family."

One part of her wanted desperately to go out with him, but another more sensible part told her that nothing could ever come of anything between Matt Crow and her. And even if they got together for a brief fling, it could cause awkwardness in the family later. Eve remembered a painful experience a few years before when she'd dated her friend Amy's brother. When the romance fizzled, things were never the same between Amy and her again.

"Eve?"

"Yes?" *Simply tell him nicely that you have other plans,* she told herself, but she couldn't make the words come out.

"Is it Charlie who's the problem?"

"Charlie?" Suddenly she remembered that Matt

assumed the Charlie she lived with was a man. Praying that God wouldn't strike her dead for another little white lie, she said, "Yes. I'm not sure that he would approve. He's jealous, extremely jealous, but thanks for calling. I have to run. My—my bathwater's running over." She quickly hung up the phone and slumped back into the chair.

Charlie Chan, the half-Siamese, half-mystery cat who was the unofficial ruler of the house, hopped on the table beside her and sat regally, waiting for her attention.

Eve scratched Charlie's head. "Hey, fellow, how did your day go? Mine has been a bummer. Do you think Matt Crow thought I was a nut case?"

The cat cocked his head. *"Meow."*

"Yeah, he probably did. But seeing him again would be *very* unwise. He would break my heart, Charlie. And if he broke my heart, my mother would know and then Irish would be upset and drag Kyle into it, and he would be in an awkward position because they are cousins and very close. No, Charlie, it's better this way."

But if it was better, why did she want to cry?

When the answering machine came on again, Matt cursed and slammed down the phone. It had taken him three days to gut up enough to call Eve; now he'd been calling every hour from six to midnight for the past three nights. After that first conversation, he'd gotten her machine every time. That was a hell of a long bath she was taking.

After he'd left Ohio, he'd tried to convince himself that Eve was taken and to stay away from her, get her out of his mind. He hadn't had any luck. She plagued his thoughts; she invaded his dreams; she haunted his senses.

He couldn't think of a single woman who could hold a candle to her. Despite her beauty, she seemed totally lacking in conceit. Instead of arrogance, she radiated genuineness and caring, even shyness. There was an inner beauty about Eve that was more dazzling than the outer.

Matt just couldn't forget her.

To hell with Charlie, he'd finally decided. It was every man for himself, and Matt meant to fight for her. He knew what it was to fight for what you wanted, and Matt had never wanted anything in his life like he wanted Eve Ellison.

Eve couldn't care that much for old Charlie and have kissed Matt the way she did. That was what gave him hope. And Charlie wasn't taking very good care of Eve, or she wouldn't be so frazzled. There were problems in that relationship; Matt was sure of it. And he intended to take advantage of those problems.

He drummed his fingers on the telephone. Something didn't ring true about that phone conversation with Eve on Wednesday. She'd seemed jumpy. Nervous? Scared? He wondered if that jerk had been listening? Is that why she wouldn't take his other calls?

"Jealous," she'd said. "Extremely jealous." Was Charlie abusive to her? Fury shot through him. If that bastard harmed one beautiful blond hair on Eve's sweet head, Matt would break his kneecaps.

Frustrated that he couldn't get through to Eve directly, Matt knew he had to figure out another way. He drummed his fingers some more and began to devise a plan.

While water boiled for pasta, Eve listened to the messages on her answering machine. The first was from her mother and father, who had just returned from a trip to Texas.

"Your dad and I fell in love with the country around Pete's place," Beverly Ellison said. "Al has definitely decided to retire, and we've bought some land there. We'll be moving to Texas soon. Call me, and I'll tell you the details."

Eve sighed. Even though she didn't make it home to Akron more than a couple of times a month, she was going to miss having her parents less than an hour's drive away. Her mom was great about dropping in with a chocolate cake occasionally, and she could always be counted on to care for the animals if one of her regular sitters wasn't available.

First Irish, now her folks. Everybody was deserting her for Texas. What was so darned great about that place anyhow?

The next message was from Lottie Abrams, a headhunter who she heard from occasionally. "Eve, give me a call the minute you get in. A really hot agency in Dallas has seen your book and is very interested in talking to you. It's a creative director's position and at twice your salary. This could be a big break for you."

Dallas? As in Texas?

Her heart gave a little trip. The image of a tall, handsome man with a cleft chin and a dynamite smile flashed into her mind. Matt Crow lived in Dallas.

Eve shook off the turn of her thoughts, but Matt's face crept back despite her efforts. He was a hard man to forget. A huge bouquet of yellow roses had arrived soon after they had talked. For three days, he'd left messages on her answering machine, each one more urgent than the last. She had deliberately ignored his calls. He must have finally gotten the hint because she hadn't heard a word from the tall Texan in a while.

She sort of missed the attention.

No. Forget Matt Crow; he was a lost cause. Certainly not her type—whatever her type was.

But Dallas was where Irish would be living. Her parents would be only a couple of hours' drive away. She was going to have to move anyway, and Dallas had lots of room. Maybe she could find a place with a barn. And, dear Lord, how she longed to work for an exciting ad agency instead of the deadly dull place where she was now.

Eve was a darned good art director, and she'd won her share of awards in the last few years, but the agency where she worked was on the skids. She'd had some ideas for turning things around if she'd gotten the promotion. But now...well, if she didn't make a move soon, her career would be in the toilet.

Creative director?

Twice her salary?

Talk about perfect timing. This could be—

Hold it, Eve, she told herself, laughing. This sounded too good to be true. There had to be a catch. It wasn't the first time that Lottie had gotten her

pumped up over some opportunity only to find that
things weren't nearly so terrific as Lottie had proclaimed.

Eve shrugged. But it wouldn't hurt to check it out.
She wouldn't even mention it to her family yet.
Fighting the urge to cross her fingers, she reached
for the phone.

Two days later, Eve was in Dallas. She couldn't
believe her luck. Coleman-Walker was becoming
well-known in the business as an innovative agency
and a real up-and-coming contender. In fact, Lottie
had sent her a couple of trade articles about the shop,
and Eve had read them on the plane. If she'd been
impressed with what she'd read, she was doubly impressed when she arrived.

From the minute she walked through the double
doors and into the funky renovated factory, Eve
knew that this would be a fantastic shop to work in.
The place was *alive*, teeming with vitality. Unmis-
takable creative energy hummed in the air and
bounced off the walls. She immediately caught the
mood of the dozen or so people she spotted; she felt
revved up and excited and broke into a grin when a
guy on roller skates whizzed by. Godzilla would
have croaked.

She loved the agency; she felt an immediate rap-
port with Bart Coleman who interviewed her. They
talked nonstop for over an hour. Working for Coleman-Walker would be a dream come true. This was
a sharp group. She ached to be a part of it.

When Bart said that the job was hers if she wanted
it, she almost burst with excitement. She wanted to

throw herself into his arms and yell, "I'll take it! How much do I have to pay you to work here?" She managed to play it cool and promised to get back with him.

Once outside the building, she couldn't hold in her excitement any longer. She threw back her head and shouted, "Yaaa-hooo!" When people turned to stare at her, she only laughed and waved and scooted around in a tight circle, pumping her arms and grinning.

No way could she turn this down. The gods had definitely smiled on her. This was the chance of a lifetime. Eve was convinced this was her destiny when she found a perfect place to live near the Dallas County line.

The elderly gentleman who owned the small farm, complete with a fixer-upper house, pecan trees, barn and chicken coop, had gone to live in a nursing home. His son had agreed to sell the property at a bargain if she would take the place "as is" and agree to care for the old gent's beloved mule and aging milk cow. A teenager from down the road had been tending them and would probably be available to help Eve if she wanted to hire him.

Why not? What were another couple of animals? She agreed at once and signed the papers. Granted, the farmhouse was a bit run-down, but a little paint would do wonders for it. The barn and the fences were in good shape. Why, she might even get a horse. She'd always wanted a horse.

This was great. Life was good. She called Bart Coleman from the airport and accepted the job—on one condition. She needed help in transporting her animals to Texas.

Matt Crow sat in his big leather chair in downtown Dallas, ankles crossed, the heel of one boot resting on the massive desk in his office. He tossed paper wads into the wastebasket and stared at the framed eleven-by-fourteen of an angel. He'd bought the picture from Irish's wedding photographer, and it had held a prime place on his desk since then. Another copy was on his dresser at home.

Would that phone never ring?

He ripped another sheet from the legal pad, wadded it, and sailed it toward the overflowing basket. He was nervous. He must have gone through half a dozen pads waiting for Bart Coleman to call. He was going to get an ulcer if this went on much longer.

The phone rang. Matt grabbed the receiver and answered before the first ring finished.

"It's a done deal," Bart Coleman said.

Matt broke into a broad grin. "She accepted?"

"Yep. Coleman-Walker has a new creative director. She reports for work on the fifteenth."

"Then the Crow Airline account is yours under the terms we discussed. But, Bart, I swear to God—"

Bart laughed. "If she ever gets wind of this, my ass is grass."

"You got that right. And I don't want Jackson or any of the rest of my family to know anything about it, either."

"Don't worry, Matt. This is strictly between you and me. And by the way, I'm impressed with the

lady and her book. I think she'll work out fine, and
if she doesn't—''

''I know. In two weeks, you say?'' He felt himself
grinning like a fool.

Three

"**S**ettled in?" Bart Coleman asked as Eve entered his office carrying a large stack of applicants' portfolios.

"Almost. I've culled these books from the ones you left on my desk. They're not bad, but the others are great." She set the load on a table and sat down across from Bart. "Sure we only need three extra people? I've found a mountain of talent already."

"Three for now. Bryan Belo, along with Sam Marcus, Nancy Brazil and a couple of freelancers are already doing some preliminary work on the new account that I want you to supervise. I don't think that you've met Bryan. He's out of town. I'll introduce you later."

"Great. I've already met briefly with Nancy and Sam, and I'm anxious to begin. Tell me about this account. Nancy said it was some sort of funky airline. That sounds almost like an oxymoron to me. I'm not sure I'd want to fly on a funky airline.''

Bart laughed. ''Don't worry about that. Although it's a small company compared to some of the big boys, Crow Airlines has always had a reputation of being safe and dependable—but fun. Wild uniforms and crazy ads, that sort of thing.''

Eve's heart lurched. *Crow?* As in Jackson Crow. As in *Matt Crow?* Surely not. ''*Crow* Airlines?'' she managed to say.

''That's right. You probably haven't heard much about the company in your neck of the woods, but getting that account was a real coup for our little shop. Not only is it an agency's dream in regard to creative possibilities, but we've been able to almost double our billing. We're about to pop our buttons. And I want you to be our number one gal in coming up with an outstanding campaign and keeping the client happy.''

Bart's excitement was evident, but her stomach felt queasy. She swallowed, then took a deep breath. ''Exactly who is the client?''

''Crow Airlines. I thought I said that.''

''Oh, you did.'' A dozen thoughts sizzled through her brain, each more ominous than the other. *Please, dear God, don't let it be one of Kyle's cousins.* Eve didn't think she could stand it if she'd gotten this terrific new job only because she was Irish's sister. ''I meant…who will I be dealing with from the company?''

''The owner himself. Great guy. We were fraternity brothers at the University of Texas, and I've been twisting his arm for that account since Gene Walker and I started the agency. He finally relented." Bart grinned and winked. "I usually leave the hustling to Gene, but I'm a helluva salesman when I put my mind to it." He glanced at his watch. "We'd better get cracking. We're set to meet our new client for lunch."

When Bart strode to the door and motioned for her to precede him, she balked, every muscle in her body tense. "Who is this great guy who owns Crow Airlines? It wouldn't by any chance be…Jackson Crow, would it?"

"Jackson? Nah, not him."

Her muscles began to relax.

"It's his younger brother, Matt."

She knotted up again, and her stomach turned over. "Matt? Matt Crow?"

"Yeah. He's a great guy. You'll like him."

"I—I already know Matt."

Bart's eyebrows went up. "You do? Hey, that's fantastic!"

"He's my brother-in-law's cousin," she said, carefully watching her boss's reaction.

"His cousin?" Bart hooted and slapped his fist into his open palm. "No joke? Hot damn! This is great. Super. Wait till Gene hears this. Man, I can't believe our luck. Come on. Let's go tell him the news."

"Wait, Bart, I have to ask. Did you know that my sister's husband was related to Matt Crow? Is that why I got this job?"

"Related?" He frowned. "Absolutely not. I didn't know that you were related to anybody, and it wouldn't have mattered if you were. Having connections won't get the job done. Eve, you got this CD spot because you're a talented lady and the best person for the position. Don't doubt that for a minute. Who is your sister anyway? I don't know if I've met her.''

"Irish Ellison, the model. Or she used to be a model. She's married to Dr. Kyle Rutledge now, and living in Dallas. Kyle and Matt are cousins.''

"Irish is your sister? I've never met her, but I remember seeing her ad work. Beautiful woman.'' He cocked his head and studied Eve's face. "Now that you mention it, I can see the family resemblance. Why didn't you go into modeling?''

"Me?'' Eve snorted. "You've got to be kidding. Irish got the looks.'' She grinned. "I got the brains.''

"I'd say you got plenty of both. Let's go meet our client. Boy, have I got a surprise for him.''

Matt was nervous. He'd plucked all the petals off the daisies in the little table vase, built a fort of sugar packets, and drunk two cactus margaritas. He was about to order a third when he saw her.

God, she was gorgeous.

He was doubly thankful for the miracle of his vision now. A few years ago, before his surgery, she would have been a blur coming toward him instead of an angel on earth. He couldn't have appreciated the exquisite color of her eyes or the sensuous curve of her lips without his Coke-bottle lenses.

He didn't know if it was the tequila or something else, but when he stood, his legs felt rubbery. Craziest damned thing. His heart kicked into overdrive and his palms went damp. He hadn't felt such a staggering reaction to a female since he was fourteen and kissing Miranda Toney behind the gym. Only this was worse.

Be cool, Crow, Matt told himself. *Play this cool.* "Bart. Gene," he said, shaking hands with the men. "And this lovely lady is—Eve?"

"Eve Ellison is the new creative director for your account," Bart said. "She tells me that her sister is married to your cousin."

"Right," Matt said, taking her hand. "We met at the wedding. What a pleasant surprise to see you here. I didn't realize that you had moved to Dallas. I thought you lived in…was it Pittsburgh?"

"Cleveland."

"How's George?"

"George?"

"Your fella."

"My—? Oh, you mean Charlie?"

"Right. Charlie."

"He's fine."

"Did he move to Dallas, too?"

She nodded.

Matt clenched his teeth against the expletive that almost popped out of his mouth. Instead he said, "What will you have to drink? I can recommend the cactus margaritas. In fact, I think I'll have another one." He motioned for the waiter.

Damn that Charlie's sorry hide! Matt was hoping the man wouldn't move to Dallas with her, but no matter. Matt was determined to have Eve—Charlie or no Charlie. And when he set his mind to something, he always got what he went after.

Always.

Grandpa Pete often said that Matt was like a snapping turtle: when he got his teeth in something, he wouldn't let go. Grandpa Pete was right. All his life, Matt had been fascinated with airplanes and flying. He'd ached to learn to fly, but he couldn't pass the vision test. The first thing he'd done when he got his million from his grandfather was have laser surgery. He hadn't told a soul his plans—especially his mother—but he was determined to learn to fly. And, despite the odds against it, he had.

Somehow Matt managed to keep his mind on business during the rest of lunch—switching to coffee instead of guzzling that third margarita helped—but he wasn't able to keep his eyes off Eve. Once, when she glanced up from eating and caught him staring at her, he winked. She turned as red as the spiced tomato on her fork and quickly turned her attention back to her salad.

He grinned. Charlie or no Charlie, the chemistry was still there.

Watch out, sugar. Here I come.

The food was probably delicious—was indeed outstanding, according to Bart and Gene—but everything Eve tried to swallow seemed to get stuck in her throat. And she was suddenly painfully aware of her appearance.

Had she combed her hair? Was she wearing lipstick? She couldn't remember. She had worn a purple jacket that Irish said was a ghastly color for her and totally out of style, but since it was still serviceable, Eve hadn't tossed it as her sister had suggested. And

she was painfully aware that one of the dogs—
Gomez, she suspected—had chewed on the toe of her
left black pump. She'd covered the teeth marks rea-
sonably well with a felt marker, and, besides, she
could keep her feet under the table. But there was
nothing she could do about the jacket. She couldn't
take it off because while she was chasing Gomez
through the pasture that morning, she'd ripped the
underarm seam of her blouse and gotten a grass stain
on her elbow. She hadn't had time to change.

Anyhow, Matt Crow really wasn't interested in
her. He hadn't even recognized her at first. So much
for lasting impressions. Hers on him, not vice versa.
His face, his voice, his touch had lingered in her
mind and her heart. Now, seeing him in person again,
she realized that her memories hadn't done him jus-
tice. His charisma enveloped her with its power and
sent tendrils deep into hidden nooks of her awareness.

She felt almost naked before him.

When he'd winked at her, she knew that he knew,
and she'd felt her face flame. How could she work
with this man feeling as she did? Heaven only knew
how long she could keep from throwing herself into
his arms and saying, "Take me. I'm yours."

Thankfully Matt Crow was the president of a busy
company, and naturally he wouldn't have time to be
personally involved with every phase of the ad campaign. Eve would be working with one of his asso-
ciates, she was sure. That would be her salvation—
or else she would probably make a complete fool of
herself and embarrass the entire family as well.

After Matt signed the check, he turned to Eve,

smiled and said, "I intend to clear my calendar as much as possible so that I can be personally involved with every phase of the ad campaign. In fact, I'd like to take you to dinner tonight and discuss some of your plans."

Panic shot through her. "Dinner? Tonight?"

She glanced back and forth between Bart and Gene. Bart was smiling expectantly. Gene was smiling expectantly. She glanced at Matt.

Matt was smiling expectantly.

"Yes," he said. "Dinner. Tonight. I'll pick you up at your office, and we can have drinks first."

"Uh, well, uh...I have animals."

"Good, I like animals. What time shall I pick you up?"

"I can't...I mean...I have to go home and feed the animals. You see, being in a new place makes them nervous, and...well, I had to lock Gomez in the barn this morning. He was chasing the neighbor's cows and making them berserk. I pray he's still there."

"Gomez?"

"He's a dog. Part golden retriever and part tunnel rat. He's a digger. The fence hasn't been made that can hold him."

Matt chuckled. "I had a dog like that once when I was a kid. Drove my mother crazy. Can't Charlie handle Gomez?"

"*Charlie?* No."

"Tell you what. You go home and tend to the animals this evening, and I'll stop by the deli and pick up some dinner. What's your address?"

"Oh, I live a long way out of town, a long way.

Almost to Forney. I wouldn't want you to drive so far."

"I like to drive," Matt said. He smiled again, and she melted like a Popsicle on hot pavement. "Give me directions."

With no other options in her mushy brain, she gave him directions to the farm.

"What does Charlie like?"

"Charlie?"

"Yes. I thought I'd bring enough food for him. He like pasta?"

Blood drained from her face. A feeling of impending doom filled her. He was going to find out that she had lied. "Fish. Charlie likes fish."

Four

Heavy rain pelted the windshield like hailstones. Eve leaned forward and squinted, trying to see the highway through the slap of the wipers. Even though she'd left the office in plenty of time to get home, feed the animals and freshen up, she hadn't counted on the jack-knifed moving van that had blocked two lanes and caused a humongous snarl. Or on the sudden deluge from the sky. Traffic inched along.

Matt Crow was due at the farm in fifteen minutes. No way would she be home by then. Her stomach knotted tighter. She gripped the steering wheel, peered at the endless strings of red lights in front of her, and worried about her animals. They were bound to be wet and hungry. Hopefully they'd taken shelter on the porch or under the barn's shed.

She was particularly concerned about Lonesome

and Sukie, the old mule and cow that had come with the place. Lonesome was half-blind and Sukie needed to be milked. They were used to going to the barn in the evening, but she'd locked Gomez inside that morning, not thinking that she would be so late getting home.

Eve turned on the radio, trying to find some music to soothe her jangled nerves.

It didn't help.

After what seemed like hours, she finally made it to the outskirts of Dallas, past Mesquite, which abutted the city, then onto open highway. The traffic thinned, and she was able to increase her speed. Home wasn't far now.

A few minutes later, she turned onto the rutted drive to the farm and bumped over the cattle guard. Her headlights swept over a sleek black sports car parked by the front gate.

"Oh, no," she moaned. "He's here." How had Matt made it through the same traffic she'd been cursing? She didn't have time to worry about that now, she thought as she pulled to a stop beside him.

As soon as she threw open the door, Matt was there with a golf umbrella and a large flashlight. "I figured you got stuck in traffic," he said.

"I did, and you'll have to excuse me. I have to see about the animals. Poor Lonesome and Sukie are locked out of the barn. And Gomez must be having a fit. Sorry, you'll have to come back another time."

Ignoring the downpour, she dashed through the front gate, out the back gate and toward the barn where the vapor light had come on. The dogs had begun barking like crazy and ran after her, circling and dancing around as if it were a game.

"I'll help," Matt yelled.

"Come back another time!" She half turned to wave him off, stumbled, and took a header into a deep puddle. The dogs splashed around her, licking and nudging, wanting to play. "Stop it, you guys. Back to the house. Now!" Thankfully, they obeyed.

Mumbling, she pushed herself to her feet and wiped the mud from her face. She was covered with guck. Irish wouldn't have to worry about the purple jacket again. It was ruined.

She squinted toward the barn door. Things looked very blurry, even accounting for the rain and the poor lighting. Blast! Her contact lens must have popped out. Knowing that it was a lost cause, still she knelt on the ground and patted around in the mud.

"Are you hurt?" Matt asked, squatting beside her and holding the big umbrella over them.

"I'm fine." Embarrassed to be caught in such a predicament, she hurriedly pushed herself to her feet and made another swipe at her muddy face. "Listen, this isn't a very good time for us to talk. Things are kind of hectic around here now. Let's make it another time." Keeping one eye closed, she dashed for the barn.

Sukie and Elmer, quietly ignoring each another, stood under the shed. Lonesome stood shivering in the rain, waiting at the barn door. Eve felt lower than a worm.

"Poor baby," she crooned, patting the sad old mule. "I'll have you dry and comfortable in just a minute." She unlatched the door and held it wide.

The mule ambled inside, then she called to the cow and goat, and they followed.

"How can I help?"

Eve started at the sound of Matt's voice. "I thought you'd gone. Sorry, I really do have too much to do to entertain tonight." She picked up a handful of rags and started to dry Lonesome.

"I don't have to be entertained, and you have to eat sometime. The food's in a cooler in the car, so it'll keep. I'll be happy to help. Just tell me what you need done."

She sighed. Lord, she must look a fright, but the animals were more important than her appearance. "Okay. Why don't you finish drying Lonesome, and I'll milk Sukie. Elmer's pretty sturdy and independent, so he'll be okay. Then maybe you can feed Winston Churchill and Louie and—Gomez!" She quickly scanned the barn, squinting to focus with her good eye. "Where is Gomez? I left him inside, and now he's gone."

"Gomez?" Matt asked, taking the rags to wipe Lonesome. "Oh. Gomez, the digger dog."

Sukie moved around her stall restlessly and gave a plaintive bawl.

"I know, sweetie," Eve said to the cow. "I'll be there in just a sec. Oh, dear," she said to Matt. "There's no telling what Gomez is up to. I hope he's not terrorizing the neighbor's cattle again."

"Want me to go look for him?"

She shook her head. "I'll have to find him. Can you handle things here?"

"Sure. What's to do?"

"Throw a blanket over Lonesome and milk Sukie." She started for the door.

"Milk Sukie?"

She nodded. "The pail and stool are over there. Can you do that?"

"Sure," Matt told her, and she hurried out the door, shouting for the dog. "No problem."

"Sure I can," Matt told himself as he threw a blanket over the bony old mule.

"No problem." He shucked his silk sports coat and tossed it over a rail, then rolled up his shirt-sleeves. He picked up the bucket in one hand and the stool in the other and went to the cow's stall.

"Evenin', Sukie. I've come to milk you."

The cow swung her head around and perused him with her big brown eyes. He could have sworn that he heard her sigh. Must have been animal instinct. Truth was, he didn't know how to begin to milk a cow, and he hadn't fooled her for one minute.

Well, that wasn't exactly true. Matt did know how to begin. He'd seen cows milked in movies, he supposed, and one summer when he was about eight, Grandpa Pete had tried to teach him. As he recalled, that cow had kicked him and stepped on his foot. He'd limped for a week.

Matt sat down on the stool and placed the bucket under the udder. "Okay now, sweetheart, let's give this a shot. If you'll cooperate, I'd appreciate it. And just so you understand my position, if you step on my foot, I'm going to whomp your rump with a two-by-four."

The cow stood very still.

So far, so good.

Matt rubbed his hands together and blew on his fists to warm his fingers, then grabbed a teat in each hand and squeezed.

Nothing happened.

He tried it again.

Not a dribble.

"Sukie, honey, you don't seem to be cooperating here."

The cow swung her head around again. He could have sworn that she rolled her eyes.

After about five minutes of squeezing and yanking and cursing, Matt hadn't produced more than a drop or two in the bucket, but he'd worked up a sweat. Bad as he hated it, he had to admit that he was stymied. And the last thing he wanted was to look like a damned fool in front of Eve.

Patting Sukie's flank, he said, "Hang on a minute, old gal. I have to call in a consultant."

He retrieved his cell phone from his jacket and punched in Grandpa Pete's number. Thank God his grandfather was home.

Matt explained his predicament to his grandfather, and when Pete quit cackling with laughter, he said, "Okay, son, now here's what you do..."

When Eve returned to the barn, soaking wet and shivering, she found Matt Crow, president of Crow Airlines, sitting on a stool and singing. His spirited, though slightly off-key, rendition of "Old MacDonald Had a Farm" filled the barn as he milked Sukie to the animated rhythm of his new words: "A squirt-squirt here and a squirt-squirt there, here a squirt, there a squirt, everywhere a squirt-squirt—"

He glanced up from his task and smiled in that special way of his. Oh, what a smile that was. It warmed her through.

"Find Gomez?" he asked.

She swiped at her dripping face and nodded. "He's warm and dry at a neighbor's house, being charming and mooching roast beef for dinner. They'll keep him until morning. And I fed Winston Churchill and Louie and Dewey. Are you about finished?"

"I have half a bucket. I think that's about it."

She glanced into the pail. "That's better than I usually do. I'd never milked a cow in my life until last week. Jimmy Johnson, a teenager from the next farm, taught me. I didn't think to ask if you knew how, but with your boots and all, well, I simply assumed that you knew something about cattle. Jimmy said that everybody around here learns how to milk a cow when he's a kid. I felt like a total doofus because I was so ignorant." She grinned. "Obviously, you're an expert. When did you learn?"

Matt picked up the pail and patted Sukie's rump. "Oh, I believe the first time I tried it, I was about eight. Tell me, who are Winston Churchill and Louie and Dewey?"

"Winston Churchill is a rooster. Louie and Dewey are ducks."

"Where's Huey?"

"Huey didn't make it much past Easter. Live chicks and ducklings are lousy gifts for three- and four-year-olds, especially city kids."

"I agree. Little pink and blue fluff-balls grow up. How did you come by them?"

"I'm a natural-born sucker." She shivered.

"We need you get you inside and out of those wet clothes."

At unbidden images of Matt slowly removing her sodden garments, heat flashed over her, and the shivering stopped abruptly. Surely, he didn't mean.... Her breath held, she searched his face for any sign that he was thinking what she was thinking.

His expression was totally innocent. Except for a tiny twitch of a dimple.

"Come on," he said. "You need to change."

As soon as she made sure that the animals in the barn had everything they needed, Eve led Matt to the house through the pounding rain. Even though she couldn't get any wetter, Matt insisted that she hold his big golf umbrella over the two of them while he carried the milk.

"You're going to let a *pig* in your house?"

Eve smiled as she toweled off the little pot-belly. "Shhhh. Minerva doesn't know that she's a P-I-G. Anyhow, she's much neater than any of the dogs. Brighter, too."

Minerva grunted in agreement.

Matt gave Charlotte, the Saint Bernard, a pat while Lucy and Bowie, a pair of large mixed-breed strays she'd adopted as puppies stood patiently waiting.

Eve held open the front door for Minerva and the dogs that Matt had helped her to dry. "Let me fix their food, then I'll clean up and we can have dinner."

He followed her into the wide hall that ran down the center of the house, and when a rich tenor voice sang out, "*Caro nome chel il mio cor,*" he stopped dead. "Charlie?"

She laughed. "No. That's Caruso. He's a myna."

"As in bird?"

She nodded. "His cage is in the living room. I hope you like opera. Sometimes he's quiet, but other times, when he feels like singing, he won't shut up. His former owner was a rather neurotic voice coach."

"How did you come by him?"

"Well, Sergio, his owner, died. A stroke. He was eighty-two and a very sweet old man. He and Caruso lived in the apartment across the hall from me, and…well, Sergio left Caruso to me in his will. You see, Caruso has some special problems and Sergio's sister absolutely couldn't abide him, so—" She shrugged.

"So his sister got the couch and the piano, and you got the bird."

Eve grinned. "Something like that."

"*Ri-di, Pagliaccio,*" the voice sang. "*Ah-ha-ha-ha!*"

Matt chuckled. "Maybe I can teach him a little Mark Chestnut, George Strait or Neal McCoy."

"Who are they?"

Looking abashed, Matt said, "You've never heard of George Strait?"

"Maybe. Isn't he a singer?"

"The best. I can see that I need to work on some holes in your education. You can't live in Texas and not know about George or Mark or Neal. They're country singers—and, more importantly, Texas boys. Don't you have any honky-tonks in Cleveland?"

"Not that I know about. At least I've never been to a honky-tonk." She reached down to pat and shush Bowie and Lucy who were dancing around impatiently.

"If you had been, you'd know it. I'll take you boot scootin' at the Red Dog one night. Now you go change out of those wet clothes before you catch cold. I'll feed this hungry crew."

"Thanks. Their food is in the pantry. I'll—" Eve looked down at the wet puddle she'd stepped in. "Okay, guys, which one of you did this?"

"Wasn't me," Matt said.

She laughed. "I didn't think so."

He looked up. "Looks like you've got a leak."

"A leak? Oh no. Let me get a pot from the kitchen."

There was another puddle in the kitchen.

"Oh, blast," Eve said. "The roof's like a sieve." She mopped up the puddles, and Matt put a roaster on the floor of the hall and a stew pot beside the old gas stove. They found two more leaks in the living room, another in the hall and one in the front bedroom. Thankfully her bedroom seemed okay when she checked it. Turning to leave, she crashed into Matt, who had followed her into the room.

"Whoops," he said, laughing as he grabbed her shoulders. "Easy there, darlin'."

"Sorry. I—" Words fled as she looked up into Matt's face. That pesky heat flushed over her again, and she grew excruciatingly aware that they were standing alone in her bedroom.

Eve wasn't accustomed to having men in her bedroom, especially not a man like Matt, who set her heart racing and her imagination conjuring up erotic scenarios. *Careful, Eve,* she told herself. *This man could tempt you into doing something foolish. And he could break your heart.* She willed her feet to move, but her feet ignored her command. Suddenly, she could think of nothing but the bed, which seemed to grow larger as she glimpsed it from the corner of her eye.

"Eve." His voice sounded husky, incredibly sexy.

"Yes?"

He smiled. "Just 'Eve.' I like the sound of your name."

"You do?"

"I do."

His face moved a fraction of an inch closer to hers and she panicked. Hurriedly, she pushed away and rushed from the room, chattering about inane trivialities to cover the awkwardness of the moment.

To the hollow tunes of drips hitting pots, Eve mentally calculated her bank balance. A new roof was out of the question. After the down payment on the farm and the plumbing repair and the new hot-water heater, her money was tight.

Oh, well, she'd just have to watch the weather forecasts for a while. If there was a chance of rain, she could set out the pots.

Leaving Matt to feed Minerva and the dogs and confine them to the sleeping porch at the back of the house, Eve took a quick shower and dressed in sweats. Since she didn't have an extra contact lens, she put on her glasses. Irish had told her they were outdated, the wrong shape for her face, and downright ugly. She frowned into the mirror and considered leaving them off, but she'd probably walk into doors and look even more stupid.

As she sat on her bed to put on her socks, she located another leak.

Her bed was wet. She jumped up quickly and looked at the ceiling. Water trickled down the light fixture overhead, and the drops fell squarely in the middle of her quilted spread.

"Great. Just great," she grumbled as she stripped off the covers and stuck a plastic wash pan under the drip. As the drops *plop-plopped* into the pan, she felt the mattress. Thank heavens it was barely damp.

Looked like she would have to spend Saturday on the roof with a hammer and patches.

After she finished towel-drying her long hair, Eve followed an enticing scent into the kitchen.

"Something smells heavenly," she said. "What—" She halted.

Matt was just lighting a candle. The table was set with a cloth, napkins and a small bouquet of yellow roses. He turned and flashed that smile. Their eyes met and held. For a moment they were encased in a bubble of intensified awareness that shut out everything but the two of them.

Her breath caught.

Soft wisps of longing slithered between them and around them, drew them deeper into a subliminal place where enchantment dwelt. Magic filled the air, flashed like fireflies, hummed like a tuning fork.

"Damn!" Matt's eyes left hers, and the spell was broken. He flung away the match that had burned his fingers.

The moment became awkward for her. She knelt

and picked up the cat twining about her feet. "Hello, Charlie. I'll bet you're hungry, too."

"*Charlie?*"

"Charlie Chan. Though I don't know why he's called that. He's part Siamese, not Chinese, but he was named when I got him a couple of years ago." The cat squirmed and she put him down.

"A couple of— *That's* Charlie? *The* Charlie?"

Ooops. Her face heated. She'd been caught. She considered trying to talk her way out of her predicament, but she decided against it. The rascal in question was shamelessly rubbing against Matt's ankles and meowing.

She sighed. "That's Charlie. *The* Charlie. He must smell the fish."

Matt had gone very still, and his dark eyes seemed to bore into her. "Do you mean to tell me that the Charlie you live with is a *cat?*"

Eve swallowed back the constriction in her throat. "Last time I looked, he was," she said, trying to keep things light. Matt didn't smile. "Are you angry, Matt?"

He sucked in a deep breath. "Angry? No. Stunned is more like it. And damned relieved if you want the truth." He shook his head, then laughed and scooped up the cat. "Hello there, buddy. I'm very glad to make your acquaintance. You like fish, do you? How about some smoked salmon?"

Charlie bumped Matt's chin with his head and purred like a motorboat.

Even Pansy ventured out from her refuge under Eve's bed and joined them in the kitchen.

Eve picked up the old calico and stroked her gently. "Did you smell the salmon too, Pansy?"

Pansy purred loudly as well.

"You're a big hit with the animals," Eve told Matt.

Matt grinned. "It's a start, but I'm more interested in being a hit with their mistress. Can I tempt you with some salmon, too?"

"I'm a vegetarian."

"Irish told me you didn't like meat so I brought lots of vegetables. Asparagus vinaigrette. Potato salad. Sauteed mushrooms. Broccoli with hollandaise. Corn souffle. There's basil and sun-dried tomatoes on the pasta. And I brought French bread. It's in the oven warming with some of the other stuff."

"Mmmmm. Sounds yummy. Smells fantastic."

He reached for a tress of her hair and wound it around his finger. "I love your hair. It's like moonbeams."

Her throat caught; her mind went blank. She looked into his dark eyes, and a prickling sensation flashed through her breasts. His eyes, his scent, his body heat were like a magnet drawing her to him. She glanced at his mouth. It was a lovely mouth. Full. Lips slightly parted. Unbelievably sensual.

He tugged gently on the strand of hair entwined on his finger. She leaned toward him, mesmerized by his mouth.

When his lips touched hers, they were soft.

Warm.

She purred and moved closer to the source of such exquisite sensation.

With a *yeow* and a hiss, both cats protested loudly and began to wiggle and squirm.

Matt and Eve jumped apart as the cats flew from their arms.

"Damnation!"

"Ouch!" Eve yelped when the strand of hair Matt held was almost pulled from its roots.

"Wait! Wait! It's tangled. Don't move."

Eve felt like an idiot, bending her head over until Matt could free her hair.

When it was loosed, Matt looked sheepish. "Sorry about that. I guess the moment is lost."

Eve bit back laughter. "The moment is lost. Let's eat." He hadn't even mentioned her glasses.

Five

"*How* much?" Eve asked, glaring at the telephone in her office as if it were something nasty. When the roofing company restated the estimate, she said, "You're kidding."

Unfortunately the man had no sense of humor. He was dead serious. A new roof would cost *thousands* of dollars. "Ma'am, I could probably patch it for a few hundred, but I couldn't guarantee it. That old roof has had it. You need a new one. Bad."

"Thanks. I'll get back to you." She called the other two companies who had promised bids. One hadn't gotten around to checking it out; the other offered a price even higher than the first. She buried her face in her hands.

"Problems?"

She glanced up and saw Sam Marcus, one of her

favorite team members. "Not until it rains. Do you happen to know what the weather report is for the next few days?"

"Sure do. Partly cloudy and mild with a seventy percent chance of thunderstorms on Sunday. I happen to know because my fiancée wants to go to Canton this weekend. She's into antiques, and once a month Canton has trading days. Hordes of people come from hundreds of miles away. It's the mother of all flea markets. She's gotten some good buys there."

"*Seventy* percent chance?"

"Yep. Looks like Canton's out on Sunday." He grinned. "Guess I'll have to watch the ball game."

"Seventy percent chance?"

"Seventy percent. You have something special planned?"

"My hammer and I have a date with the roof. It leaks. Say, you have a hammer?"

"Don't look at me, boss. I have acrophobia. If I get higher than a two-step ladder, I panic. Wimpy, I know, but that's my only failing."

"Drat!"

Sam handed her a folder. "See what you think of these before I give them to production."

"Newspaper ads for the special fares?"

Sam nodded. "And before you ask, Nancy doesn't know one end of any tool from the other, but her brother's a pretty fair mechanic if your car breaks down."

"I'll keep that in mind." Eve looked at the rough sketches. "These are great. Good job, Sam. And tell Nancy I love her copy."

"I think she'd rather hear it from you. Despite all her bravado, she likes a compliment now and again."

"Don't we all? Ask production to put a rush on it. I'd like to get these approved and running ASAP."

"Will do."

When Sam had gone, Eve glanced at her watch, then called Bryan Belo, another member of the Crow Airlines team. She'd asked him to have two thirty-second radio spots ready first thing this morning. It was almost noon.

"B.B. here. Start talking."

"This is Eve, Bryan. Have you finished the radio copy for Crow?"

"Sure thing."

"Would you bring it to my office?"

"Can't do that."

Startled, she said, "I beg your pardon?"

"I said I can't do that."

"You want to explain why not?"

"They're on Bart's desk, and he's in conference with a client."

"Why are they on Bart's desk?"

"Because he's my boss."

She could almost hear a smirk in Bryan Belo's voice, and anger flashed through her. *Stay cool,* she told herself. For some reason the senior writer disliked her intensely, and his feelings were thinly veiled. She couldn't let him get the upper hand or she was lost as an effective manager.

"So am I, Bryan," she said quietly. "You need to remember that. I presume you have the copy on your computer. Locate it, print it out, and be in my office, material in hand, in ten minutes.'' She hung up before either of them had a chance to say more.

Except for a couple of minor skirmishes with Bryan Belo and his surly attitude, Eve's first week at Coleman-Walker had been terrific. She liked the office, the people, her work. She was also falling in love with Texas. Even strangers were friendly.

Everything in Texas was bigger than life—especially a certain guy who she was growing very fond of. She'd seen Matt every day since she'd begun work. He was always dropping by for one reason or another and taking her to lunch or to dinner or for drinks—much more than was necessary for a client to do. In fact, his attention was getting a bit embarrassing around the office—not that anybody had said anything, but people noticed.

And soon they were going to be in each other's pockets for several days. Matt had insisted that they travel on Crow Airlines to some of their major service cities so she could get a real feel for his company's unique business and philosophy, he'd said. A reasonable suggestion, she supposed, but thinking about spending so much time with him made her antsy.

Her phone rang. *Speak of the devil.*

''What are you doing for lunch?'' Matt asked.

''Sam, Nancy and I are grabbing sandwiches and going to someplace called Pioneer Plaza. They wanted to show me the sculpture there.''

''Great. I like Pioneer Plaza myself. Tell you what, I'll get the sandwiches and meet you there at about twelve-fifteen.''

''But Sam and Nancy—''

"No problem," Matt said. "I'll bring plenty for everybody. I've been wanting to get to know them better, and we can bounce around some ideas about the account."

She was in a darned awkward position, but what could she say? He was the client. "Twelve-fifteen."

Bryan Belo stepped into her office as soon as she hung up. He tossed a sheaf of paper on her desk.

"The radio spots?"

"Yeah," he said. "That all?" He turned to leave without waiting for an answer.

"No. Wait just a moment while I look them over. Have a seat."

He didn't sit down. Instead he leaned against the door jamb and crossed his arms. Eve ignored his petulant attitude and took her sweet time reading his work. In fact, after he heaved a theatrical sigh, she read each spot twice. Slowly.

She glanced up from the pages and gave him a bright smile. "Bryan, these are really fine pieces. Excellent. I can't think of a single way to improve them. I'm sure the client will be pleased."

His sullen expression didn't change. "I do good work."

"Yes, you do. You're a talented writer."

"That all? I need to get back to something I'm working on."

Clamping her teeth together, she waited a moment to reply. She sensed that challenging him about his attitude would only make matters worse. "Thanks. I'd like to get together with your team about the magazine layouts later today."

He gave a curt nod and left.

Eve slumped back in her chair and blew out an exasperated breath. Bryan was turning into a real problem. She hoped she could handle the situation without having to go to Bart.

"Wow," Nancy said when Matt began unpacking the boxes and bags he'd brought. "If that's pickled shrimp I smell, I may kiss you."

Matt grinned. "Start kissing."

When Nancy gave him a playful peck on the cheek, Eve felt herself bristle. She was surprised by her reaction. Surely she wasn't jealous. Or maybe she was. Since that night when the cats interfered, Matt hadn't attempted to kiss her again, not even playfully.

Odd, she thought. As often as they'd been together in the past week, he'd had plenty of opportunities. But instead of kissing her, he'd chucked her under the chin, touched her cheek, or winked when he said good-night. He hadn't kissed her. Not once. Maybe he'd been disappointed the first time.

The thought pained her. Although she wasn't a total innocent, truthfully she hadn't had much experience. The last guy she'd dated for any length of time didn't incite much passion in her. One of the reasons she'd broken off the relationship was that she found she'd rather kiss Minerva than Kenneth. Kenneth's lips were hard, thin and dry, not like—

Remembering the sensual feel of Matt's mouth on hers, Eve went warm all over. Although she ached to savor the sensation again, her good sense told her that having a romantic relationship with a client was sheer foolishness.

"Muffeletta?" Matt asked her. "It has avocado, egg, broccoli sprouts and some other healthy stuff." He smiled knowingly and winked.

Her face heated. Had he read her mind? No, surely not. Matt didn't have romance in mind, she told herself. He was merely being polite because of the family connection and their work relationship. Why in the world would someone like Matt Crow be interested in a plain Jane like her? He was the type to sport a Dallas Cowboy cheerleader on each arm.

Big hair, big smile, big bazooms and big eyes with long eyelashes. Glamorous, sexy, experienced. That was Matt's type. Not her. Not by a long shot. She made an exasperated face.

"No meat on it," he said, offering the muffeletta again. "I promise."

"Oh. Sure. Thanks." Eve managed a smile, took the big sandwich and sat down on one of the canvas camp stools Matt had set up beneath a live oak tree.

He'd picked a perfect spot near the old founders' cemetery atop a small bluff that overlooked the massive collection of sculpture. The day was slightly overcast and mild. A bit of a breeze rustled the plumed pampas grass on the rise, fluttered the cattails in the small pond below, and combined those sounds with the rush of cascading water to obscure city noises and transport visitors back a hundred years to the days when this was open land. According to Sam, this place was a junction of several pioneer and Indian trails, a spot where real cowboys once drove great herds of beef north to market.

Now, a string of about seventy longhorn steers, each massive body over six feet tall and cast in darkening bronze, were being driven down a trail from the bluff. The metal herd, tails switching, ambled down the sloping path bounded by limestone boulders, passed a waterfall and curved to cross a shallow stream at the bottom. Two bronze cow-hands worked to keep the long line of cattle moving in the right direction, and the mounted trail boss, his right leg hooked casually over the saddle horn, sat watching the action from a vantage point only a few feet from where Matt passed out food.

"Incredible," Eve said, unable to eat for looking. "This is amazing. The detail is marvelous. I can almost smell the cattle and the trail dust and hear the steers bawling and the men whistling. And they're so...so big. I've never seen anything like it."

"No place but Texas," Matt and Sam said at almost the same time.

Nancy laughed. "You'll soon get used to us, Eve. Texans are a breed apart."

"*Us?*" Sam said, his brows lifting. "Nance, you're from *Michigan.*"

"A technicality, an accident of birth. I got here as fast as I could, didn't I?" Nancy said to Eve, "There's a sculpture of mustangs at Las Colinas that's just as impressive as the cattle drive. Some think more so."

"Man, this is great," Sam said after taking another big bite of his enormous sandwich. "Much better than liverwurst on raisin bread. I think I'm going to like working on the Crow Airlines account."

"Liverwurst on raisin bread?" Nancy said incredulously. "How awful. Why would you even consider it?'' She popped a shrimp into her mouth, then closed her eyes as she chewed.

"Desperation. It's the end of the month. Liverwurst was all that was left in the variety pack, and Aunt Sofia gave me a loaf of her raisin bread last weekend. It's been in the fridge ever since. I hate raisins.''

"Me too,'' Matt said. ''Never could abide cookies with raisins. Or fruitcakes. Nothing in this world is more awful than fruitcake.''

"I like raisins,'' Eve said. ''And fruitcake.''

"I always thought that fruitcake was a terrible waste of good pecans,'' Nancy offered. ''Now chocolate cake—that's another story. Or fudge. That's even better.''

"Didn't Irish tell me that you have a fudge factory?'' Eve asked Matt.

Matt wiped a dab of mayonnaise from the corner of his mouth. ''*Did* have. I sold it.''

"Sold it?'' Nancy said. ''A fudge factory of your very own and you *sold* it? Lord, I'd be in heaven if I owned a fudge factory. I'd have fudge for breakfast, lunch and dinner.''

Matt laughed. ''That was the problem. It was darned good fudge, and I soon gained fifteen pounds. I had a chance to make a good profit, so I sold it.''

"Sam and Nancy did some sharp print ads for the new fares,'' Eve said to Matt. ''I brought along the preliminary sketches.''

"I'll look at them later. Enjoy your lunch. Isn't it a fine day? And a great place. I'd never thought of eating here. Whose idea was it?''

"Our bright Mr. Marcus's,'' Eve told him.

"Sam, you any kin to the Neiman Marcus bunch?" Matt asked.

Sam chuckled. "Don't I wish. My great-grandfather beat them here, but he delivered ice from the little factory he started. My father is an accountant."

Eve glanced up to see an old man in seedy clothes and a grimy red baseball cap heading toward them. He pushed a grocery cart with a wobbly, squeaking wheel, and the cart was piled high with heaven knows what. A dingy gold blanket covered the contents. His grizzled face and limp hanks of gray hair verified a long hiatus between shaves and haircuts.

One of the homeless that every city had, she suspected. Discomfited by his approach, Eve glanced away. She was ashamed of her reaction, but she never knew how to act around such people. Of course, she felt sorry for the poor souls, but she didn't know what to do beyond making a contribution to the local shelters, which she'd always done in Cleveland. She couldn't take people in the way she did animals.

"Matthew. Matthew Crow," the old man said in a merry voice. "Is that you?"

Matt looked up, then broke into a grin and stood. "In the flesh." He stuck out his hand. "How you been doing, Doc?"

"Fine. Fine. Is that roast beef I smell?"

"Sure is. And I've got an extra one. Have a seat and I'll introduce you to my friends." He offered his stool to the old man.

"No, thank you, Matthew. I can't stay, but I'd like to meet your friends."

"This is Eve Ellison, Nancy Brazil and Sam Marcus, Dr. Milstead. They all work for an advertising agency I'm doing business with."

Doc doffed his cap and nodded his mottled bald pate to the group. "Delighted. And which agency do you represent?" he asked, addressing his question to Eve.

"Coleman-Walker," she said.

"Ah, a fine shop I hear. Eugene Walker was one of my students. Did rather well playing professional football as I recall. A shame about his knees." He turned to Matt. "Roast beef you said?"

"Right here, Doc. How about some potato salad or pickled shrimp?"

"Gives me indigestion. No, just the sandwich will do nicely." He craned his neck and peered into a box. "Is that strawberry cheesecake I spy? Now I wouldn't object to a slice of that. But you must let me pay you."

Matt frowned. "Doc—"

The old man chuckled. "Oh, I don't deal in cash these days, Matthew. I barter. It's a much more sensible arrangement. I imagine something in my collection would make a suitable exchange."

"Doc—"

The old man held up his hand to end the argument. "I insist."

Matt nodded.

Doc went to his heaped cart, lifted the blanket and poked his head underneath. They watched lumps and bumps of movement. At last he withdrew with a cumbersome flesh-colored object under each arm.

"I have just the thing, Matthew. Came across this

yesterday. Look, it's fine quality and barely damaged. I suspect that a clever young man like you will find a perfect use for her. I call her Maud." He handed over a female mannequin, nude, bald and in two parts that joined at the waist. Her nose was broken off and her left arm was missing.

"Thanks, Doc." Matt stood the bottom half of the mannequin against the tree trunk and laid the top half on his stool. "Sure you won't stay and join us?"

"No. No. I'll have my lunch with Mary Ellen." The old man gestured toward the cemetery. "If you ladies and gentlemen will excuse me." He nodded politely and took the box of food Matt offered.

"Is there anything else you need, Doc?" Matt's hand touched his wallet.

"Not today, Matthew." Back straight, he strode to his cart and deposited the box beneath the blanket. He gave a wave and left pushing his grocery cart, the wobbly front wheel squeaking.

Matt stood watching, his hands in his pockets, a pensive look on his face. Eve wanted to hug him for the tender way he'd treated the scruffy old man. There wasn't a bit of pretentiousness in Matt. Besides being incredibly handsome, sexy and successful, he was truly a nice man. No wonder he'd done so much to make her feel welcome in Texas. It was his nature.

"Exactly who is that old gentleman?" Eve asked. "He seems surprisingly well-spoken. You called him Dr. Milstead?"

"Dr. Henry Milstead. Fulbright scholar. Ph.D. in economics. Brilliant man. Once he was head of his department at Southern Methodist University and lived across the street from us."

"What happened?"

"His wife ran off with a rodeo clown. Shocked hell out of everybody, especially Doc. He took it bad. Started hitting the booze pretty heavy and—" He shrugged.

"Who is Mary Ellen?" Nancy asked.

"His wife."

"She died?"

"Not that I know of."

Sam started to speak, then closed his mouth.

"Sometimes he finds comfort in fantasy and cheap wine," Matt said. "Anybody ready for cheesecake?"

Everybody was.

Eve served pieces to Sam and Nancy, who strolled down toward the waterfall, eating the cake with plastic forks as they walked. She sliced a large, gooey wedge for Matt who stood beside her. "What in the world are you going to do with that mannequin?"

"Maud? Oh, I don't know. I may sleep with her."

"Sleep with her?" She laughed and brought a sticky finger to her mouth.

Matt caught her wrist. "Yep," he said quietly. "Unless I can find somebody who's a lot softer and warmer."

She watched, mesmerized, as he drew her finger to his mouth and licked the strawberry confection from it.

"Interested?" he asked.

Six

When the alarm rang at six o'clock on Saturday morning, Eve slapped it off and fought a serious temptation to return to the wonderful dream she was having, one that was deliciously erotic. A cold wet nose nuzzled her cheek, then woofed softly in her ear. Toenails clicked and danced across the oak floor. A pig squealed. The scent of coffee brewing in the automatic pot wafted in and teased her nose. The opening strains of a Wagner aria pierced her brain and popped open her eyes.

Caruso was in fine form. One of these days she was going to give that sorry-looking bird to her worst enemy. Reluctantly, she heaved herself from her warm bed and grabbed her glasses.

The roof awaited.

She groaned and padded to the front door to let

the animals out, then stuck her head through the opening and squinted at the horizon to check the weather. It was clear. So far, so good.

"Mornin'," a deep voice said.

She shrieked and almost jumped out of her skin. "Matt!" She grabbed a corner of the window drape near the door in a hasty attempt to cover herself. She often slept in only a pair of lace panties. Today they were blue.

"Yes, ma'am." Dressed in worn running shoes, ragged jeans, faded Cowboys T-shirt and a Texas Rangers cap, he was leaning back in the old hide-bottomed straight chair with his long legs propped on the porch railing and his fingers curled around a plastic cup. His eyes sweeping over her, he grinned and stood.

Clutching the fabric to conceal her near-nudity, she poked her head out the opening. "What are *you* doing here?"

"I brought my hammer. I thought you might need some help with the roof."

"Thanks, but you don't need to do that. I can manage."

"No problem. Just being neighborly. Folks around these parts always like to pitch in and help. The others should be here pretty soon."

"The *others?*"

"Yep." His eyes drifted downward from her face. "You might want to get dressed. Not for me, you understand. What you're wearing suits me just fine, but..." His smile broadened.

Eve glanced down and nearly died of embarrassment. "Oh, no!" She'd grabbed the sheer instead of the heavy drapery, and she'd forgotten that the front door had a large oval glass inset. "Close your eyes," she shouted, then turned and made a dash for her bedroom.

From the rumble of laughter behind her, she knew darned well that he'd watched every moment. And enjoyed it. How could she face him again? She was tempted to hole up in her room for a year or two.

The roof.

She sighed. It had to be fixed today. And with agency connections and family ties and…other things, there was no avoiding Matt. She would simply brazen it out. Pretend that the humiliating episode had never happened.

A few minutes later, after she'd dressed in grubby clothes and pulled back her hair with a rubber band, Eve poked up the nose piece of her glasses and strode into the kitchen. She'd considered putting on makeup and her new contacts but decided against it. After all, neither would have helped her appearance that much, and she was going to fix a roof, not attend a party.

Quickly she fed the cats, grabbed a cup of coffee and a bagel, and hurried out the front door.

Matt was leaning against the porch rail. He neither smirked nor gave any indication that anything extraordinary had happened. "You ever fixed a roof before?" he asked.

Thank goodness he wasn't going to mention the episode, either. She could have hugged him.

"No, but the man at the home improvement place where I bought supplies last night gave me instructions." She pulled a folded booklet from the hip pocket of her jeans. "And this. I've read it thoroughly. Do you know much about repairing shingles?"

"A little. I worked in construction one summer when I was in college."

"Only one summer?"

"Yep. I figured out that being a lifeguard was a lot easier job. Better fringe benefits."

"Did the fringe benefits wear bikinis?"

He laughed. "How'd you guess? Let me take a look at that pamphlet."

After paging through it quickly, he said, "Got it. Where do we start?"

Eve frowned at him. "You read that?"

"Yep. I'm speedy. In most things." He tapped her nose, then leisurely traced the line of her bottom lip. "But with other things, I go very, very slowly."

She almost turned into a puddle of protoplasm and leaked through the porch cracks.

"You...you do?"

He nodded. Slowly. "Yep. And by the way, I like you in blue lace."

"Well...uh—" She cleared her throat. "I'd rather you forget what happened. It's very embarrassing. Uh... I guess we'd better get started."

He seemed fascinated by her mouth. His gaze was glued to it as his finger made a slow trail along her top lip. "It's a hard thing to forget. No need to be embarrassed. You're a beautiful woman. Just tell me what you want me to do."

"Do?" she squeaked. She cleared her throat again and tried it an octave lower. "Do?"

"Uh-huh. I'll do anything you want." His voice was as suggestive as rumpled satin sheets.

If she let this play much longer, she was going to jump his bones. Matt Crow with his dimpled chin, sin-dark eyes and killer smile was the sexiest man in Texas. In the world. In the universe.

She licked her lips. He licked his.

"Then get your hammer and follow me." She turned and marched away before she dragged him to her bed.

A horn honked and two pickup trucks bumped across the cattle guard and pulled up behind Matt's car at the gate. The dogs and Minerva bounded to the fence.

"That must be the others," Matt said.

"What others?"

"Grandpa Pete, my brother Jackson, and a couple of hands from Jackson's place. They're going to help with the roof. Kyle has surgery scheduled this morning. He said he'd be over later. Irish is supposed to bring some sandwiches."

"Mornin'," Pete Beamon said, waving to Eve and Matt as he climbed out of one of the trucks. "Who's bringing sandwiches?"

"Irish," Matt told him.

"No need for that," the old man said. "I brought chili enough for half the county. Jackson, fetch that pot to the kitchen. Jimmy, you and Buddy set the coolers on the porch."

Jackson Crow grinned at Eve and tugged the brim of his weathered cowboy hat. "Mornin', Eve. Hope you like chili." His muscles strained as he hoisted a huge stainless steel soup pot from the bed of the truck. "Which way's the kitchen?"

"Come on, I'll show you," Matt said. "And careful you don't scare Pansy."

"Who the hell's Pansy?" Jackson asked as he strode up the front steps with the pot.

"Ri-di, Pagliaccio!"

"Is that Pansy?" Jackson asked.

"Nope," Matt said. "That's Caruso."

Eve held out her hand to the old man, who looked more comfortable dressed in overalls than the tux he'd worn to Irish's wedding. "Pete, it's good to see you."

"Good to see you too, Eve." He clasped her hand and patted it. "We're glad to have you in Texas, and it won't be long before your mama and daddy will be moving down here." Pete reached down to scratch Bowie and Gomez behind the ears. He laughed as Charlotte, Lucy and Minerva nudged their way in for some attention. "Well, what have we here? A pig?"

"Shhhh," Eve said. "Minerva doesn't know she's a pig." She clapped her hands. "Okay, guys, settle down. We have work to do."

Minerva and the dogs retreated to the porch and took their accustomed spots.

"Well-behaved animals," Pete said. "Speaks well for their owner. These boys are Jimmy and Buddy," he told her, acknowledging the men who'd joined them on the porch. "Work for Jackson at that place of his, and they're pretty fair hands at fixin' things like roofs. Yours in bad shape, is it?"

"Leaks like a sieve," Matt said as he and Jackson rejoined them.

"Well, let's take a look," Pete said. "Jackson, you get the ladder."

"Grandpa, you're not getting on that roof," Jackson said. "Matt and I will do the lookin'. You're in charge of the food and drinks. Say, didn't you bring a thermos of coffee?"

"No reason I can't get on that roof and do a day's work. My hip's all healed up good as new."

Matt and Jackson both cocked dark brows at their grandfather.

"Oh, all right," the old man groused as he stomped off. "I'll get the thermos."

"He's such a sweetheart," Eve said.

"And stubborn as a mule," added Matt. "Let's check out the roof and see what we need to do."

"This roof is in bad shape," Jackson declared.

"Terrible," Matt agreed. "And, Jackson, you're gonna break your fool neck wearing your boots up here."

"Naw," Jackson said. "These are my roofing boots. And I'm as surefooted as a mountain goat. Eve, didn't you check out the roof before you bought this place?"

"No, I bought it 'as is.' I knew that the house needed some repairs. That's why I got a bargain."

"Looks like these old shingles have been patched a dozen times," Jimmy said.

"I think you need a whole new roof, ma'am," Buddy added. "This one's about rotted through."

Eve sighed. "I can't afford a new roof right now."

"Hell, I'll buy you a new one," Jackson said.

"The devil you will," Matt shot back. "If anybody buys her a new roof, it'll be me."

Buddy snickered.

Rankled, Eve said, "I'll buy my *own* roof when I can afford it."

"Don't know why you won't let us put a new roof on for you, sugar," Jackson said. "After all, you're family, and the whole bunch of us have more money than we have sense. Shoot, I won more'n enough last night in a friendly poker game to stake you to a roof."

"Thank you, but no," she said firmly. "For now, we'll just have to patch this one as best we can. The place over the kitchen is the worst."

"About here?" Matt asked, stamping on a spot that had two or three layers of patches. "Looks—" He let out a yell when his foot went through the shingles, and he sank up to his knee.

Jackson roared with laughter. "Wanna borrow my boots?"

"Shut up, Jackson, and pull me out of this danged hole."

Eve rushed to help, as did Buddy and Jimmy. Jackson kept laughing.

"Are you hurt?" Eve asked.

Matt rotated his foot and bent his leg. "Everything seems to be working. I just tore my jeans is all."

"Matt, you're bleeding!" She knelt to check his leg. "You've got a gash."

"What in the tarnation's going on up there?" Pete yelled from below. "A hunk of the ceiling almost landed in my chili!"

"Sorry, Grandpa," Jackson shouted. "Matt's big foot went through the roof."

"You hurt, boy?"

"Naw."

"Yes, you are," Eve whispered. "I think you need stitches."

"It's just a scrape."

"It is *not* just a scrape," Eve said, irritated with Matt's macho attitude and his brother's amusement about the injury. "Jackson, there is nothing funny about this. Matt is hurt. Help me get your brother down. I'm going to take him to the emergency room."

Jackson sobered immediately. "Yes, ma'am. You really hurt, Matt?"

"Looks like a right smart of blood," Jimmy said.

Eve started issuing orders, and soon Matt was in the front seat of her utility vehicle with a towel wrapped around his leg and Kyle alerted at the hospital.

"Sure you don't want me to come along?" Cherokee Pete asked, his wrinkled face full of concern.

"Or me?" Jackson asked, solemn now.

"We'll be fine," Matt said. "I'd rather you two stay here and take care of Eve's roof. That hole I made is gonna take a *big* patch." He gave an exaggerated wink.

"Gotcha," Jackson said.

Dr. Kyle Rutledge, plastic surgeon, studied the gash on the side of Matt's calf. "It's not too bad. I'll give you a couple of my neatest stitches so that you'll have a prettier scar. When the hair grows back, you won't even be able to find it.''

"What hair? Oh, no, Kyle, you're not shaving my leg. Why don't you forget the stitches and slap a bandage on it?''

"Who's the doctor here, cousin?" Kyle asked as he cleaned the wound.

"Ouch! Dammit, that hurts. At least give me a stick to bite on.''

Kyle laughed and picked up a syringe. "How about a shot of Novocain instead?''

"Sounds good to me.'' Matt lay back on the gurney and looked away as Kyle numbed the spot. Bad as he hated to admit it, especially to one of his cousins, he hated shots of any kind. Always had.

"How long since you've had a tetanus vaccination?''

Matt shrugged. "Not long.''

"How long?''

"I don't remember.''

"That's what I thought.'' Kyle turned to the nurse. "Mrs. Maroney, when we're through here, rustle up a tetanus shot for my cousin. Use a *big* needle.''

"Dammit, Kyle!''

Kyle only laughed.

Eve tried to read a magazine, then gave up and paced. They had been gone from home a long time. First, they had to have Matt's leg X-rayed, then there were blood tests, and it seemed as if they waited forever while Kyle finished in surgery. Matt wouldn't entertain the notion of anyone but Kyle tending his wound, and since it wasn't actually life-threatening, they waited.

At last Kyle came through the door. He grinned at Eve, took her hands, and kissed her forehead. "How's my favorite sister-in-law?"

"I'm a nervous wreck. How is Matt? Was anything broken? Is he going to be okay?"

"He's fine. Nothing's broken, and I put a few dainty stitches in his leg. My nurse is giving him a couple of shots now. He only needs to take it easy for a day or two and take his medicine." He tore a sheet off a prescription pad and handed it to her. "One is an antibiotic, and the other is for pain. Maybe you could swing by the drugstore and pick them up before you head home. I think Irish is already at your house by now, and I'll be along to help soon. Don't let Matt up on the roof again today."

"I won't, Kyle. It's my fault that he got hurt. I'll see that he takes care of himself."

"I was thinking more of your roof than Matt. He's liable to stomp another hole in it." He laughed. "I'd give a hundred dollars to have seen that. I'll bet Jackson carried him high."

"He did. And I didn't think it was funny at all."

"I know, sweetheart." He kissed her forehead again. "See you later."

In a few moments, Matt came through the door in a wheelchair pushed by a very cute young aide. His jeans had been cut off at the knee, his left shoe was in his lap, and his calf sported a bandage.

After she helped Matt into her front seat, they were on their way to the drugstore.

"Do you mind swinging by my place before we

go back to your farm? I need to get another pair of pants and some clean socks. Won't take me but a minute."

"Of course I don't mind, but I feel guilty leaving the others to work alone on my roof."

"Don't worry about it. I called Grandpa before I left the emergency room to let him know I was okay. He said they were moving along just fine and not to hurry. Irish brought some sandwiches and a coconut cake and they were having a picnic. Speaking of food, I'm hungry. How about we pull in a drive-in and get a cheeseburger and some fries?"

After they picked up the medicine and the food, Matt directed her to his apartment on Turtle Creek, a very prestigious address north of downtown. She was concerned about his being on his leg too much, but they drove to an underground lot, parked by an elevator, and rode up to the penthouse with only a few steps. She insisted that he lean on her.

His apartment was spectacular. Unbelievable view; unbelievable furnishings. It fairly shouted wealth. Her modest farmhouse paled in comparison. Again she was reminded that their lifestyles were miles apart. Irish was always destined to diamonds; Eve wasn't.

Matt plunked the burger sacks on a metal-and-glass coffee table. "Make yourself at home. I'll be right back."

When Eve caught sight of herself in a large mirror, she was horrified. Her glasses really were as ugly as Irish had said. Her face was pallid without makeup, and her hair went every which way. The jersey and jeans she wore should have been thrown away years ago. For the first time, amid Matt's posh furnishings, she was truly aware of what a mess she was. She'd always known, but she'd never cared much before. It had never been important.

She scrunched up the big toe that was poking out the hole in her sneaker and wiped her hands on the seat of her jeans. She glanced around and spotted a powder room. Maybe she could at least brush her hair.

Brushing didn't help. She had the mother of bad hair days. It had lumps and bumps in all the wrong places. She ended up pulling it back again and putting the rubber band around it. She couldn't find a tube of lipstick anywhere in her shoulder bag. She rummaged through the vanity drawers and found a tube. *Wonder who this belongs to?* It was sort of a ghastly deep maroon, but she applied it anyhow.

It looked more ghastly on.

She tissued it off—or tried to. The stuff clung like grape Popsicle stain.

Oh, great! She looked worse than when she started. She sighed. Face it, Ellison. A stunner, you ain't.

She washed her hands, stuck the ugly glasses in her pocket, and went back to the living room. Matt sat on the couch in a fresh pair of jeans. He was tearing open the sacks and dividing the food—a bacon cheeseburger for him, a salad for her.

"You had the root beer, right?" He frowned. "What's wrong with your lips?"

"Don't ask." She stumbled over the glass coffee table, and Matt caught her before she fell. "Oh, drat." She blinked away the tears that stung her eyes.

"What's wrong, honey?"

"I didn't even see the coffee table."

"What happened to your glasses?"

She sighed. "They're in my pocket."

"Well, put them on."

Pulling them out, she said, "But they're so *ugly*."

Matt chuckled and put them on her. "They're not so bad. You should have seen the ones I used to wear. Now that's ugly."

"You wear glasses?"

"Not anymore, but I used to wear big heavy things that looked like telescope lenses. Kids used to tease me something fierce, but I was blind as a bat without them. I had laser surgery a few years ago, and now my vision is nearly perfect."

"Surgery?"

"Yep. I would have had it sooner, but my mother had a friend who almost lost her eyesight completely from corrective surgery, and she panicked every time I mentioned it. When I was older and the techniques improved, I decided to go for it. I'm glad I did. I was finally able to get my pilot's license."

"Did the kids really tease you?" Eve asked.

"Unmercifully. And I was considered a real nerd in high school."

Her eyes widened. *"You?"*

"Yep. Did you get teased about your glasses, too?"

"My glasses were the least of it. Everybody called me Eiffel Tower or beanpole, and nobody believed that anyone as ugly and gawky as I was could have a sister like Irish."

"Ugly and gawky? *You?*" Matt said. "I can't imagine that. You're every bit as beautiful as Irish."

"Me?" Eve snorted. "You don't have to be kind. People still don't believe we're sisters."

"I'm not being kind, and I told you my vision is nearly perfect." His brow furrowed. "Don't you know how beautiful you are?"

Eve knew she should be flattered by the compliment, but she also knew the type of man Matt was. She'd seen his kindness firsthand with Dr. Milstead. She didn't respond and silently ate her meal.

Matt seemed to have a million reasons to delay their return to the farm. When they finally drove onto her property, it was late afternoon. There were at least a half-dozen extra cars and trucks parked in front.

When they stopped, Eve let out a startled cry. "Dear heavens, what have they *done?*"

Seven

Cherokee Pete hung his thumbs in the bib of his overalls and rocked back on his heels. "Whatcha think of your new roof, Eve?"

"I'm—I'm speechless."

"Fair took my breath away, too. One of Matt and Jackson's buddies is in the construction business, and he sent out one of his crews. Said he had some extra roofing material in his warehouse, left over from a job he just finished, and he sent it along, too. I figured you wouldn't mind if it was blue. Let me tell you, that metal will last from now on. And don't nothing sound sweeter than rain on a tin roof—though I don't believe this is tin. Channel iron I recollect it's called. Purdy, ain't it?"

"It's beautiful. But it looks very expensive."

"Naw. That's the sweet part of the deal. This fellow owed the boys a favor, and it didn't cost a penny. Matter of fact, Jimmy and Buddy carried your patching stuff back to the place you bought it and swapped it for some Sheetrock and such to fix the kitchen ceiling.''

Irish came out the front door and waved. ''Hi. Come see the kitchen. I selected the color. I hope you like it. There wasn't time to do the cabinets today, but I bought extra paint for later. Kyle and Jackson are just finishing up.'' She gave Eve a hug as they entered the house. ''Matt, how's your leg?''

''Not too bad.''

Eve couldn't believe her kitchen. The stained ceiling—and its more recent hole—were covered with new plaster and painted off-white. The walls were cream.

''Like it?'' Irish asked.

''I love it. But you've done too much. How can I ever repay you?''

''Matt,'' Jackson said as he folded up a ladder, ''do something with this little Yankee gal. She keeps worrying about folks just being neighborly. Slopping a little paint on a wall is no big deal.''

''Slopping is right,'' Kyle said as he washed his hands at the sink. ''I'm glad I got here in time to do the detail work.''

''Bite your tongue, fancy doctor man,'' Jackson said. ''I'm twice the painter you are.''

''Not on your best day.''

''Hush, you two,'' Irish said, laughing. ''Come on, Kyle, we have to be at the Marshalls' party in two hours.'' She kissed Eve's cheek. ''Call you tomorrow.''

In a few minutes most everyone had gone, except Jackson and Pete. Jackson lingered on the porch, having a last beer and talking with Matt. With Gomez dogging Pete's every step, the old man insisted on helping Eve with the milking and feeding of the various animals.

"What do you do with all this milk?" Pete asked Eve as he carried the pail from the barn.

"I use what I can, but I'm afraid I have a refrigerator full. My neighbors have their own cows."

"Ever think of making butter? I'll bet I could sell all you make in my store. Truth to tell, I'm right fond of fresh, home-churned butter myself."

"That's a great idea, but I don't know how to make butter."

"Nothin' much to it. Tell you what, I've got a churn and a dasher at the trading post, and I'll have one of the boys run it up to you tomorrow. I'll have Alma Jane write out the instructions and send them along, too."

"That's great. Who's Alma Jane?"

"Lady that works in my store. She does most of the cooking—except for the chili. I make that myself."

"Really? I hear it's very...hot. Thanks for bringing it. And thanks for all the help. Despite what Jackson said, I wish there was some way that I could repay you."

"Glad to do it. A thank you is all that's needed. But I tell you what, you might do one little favor for me."

"Sure. Anything."

"I thought Matt looked a little peaked. He won't

admit it, but I think his wound is beginning to pain him some. I don't think he ought to be driving home tonight and staying by himself. I 'spect he could use some looking after for a day or two—somebody seeing that he keeps off that leg and has some nourishing meals.''

''You're absolutely right, Pete. I'll insist that he stay here in my guest room, and I can see that he eats properly and takes his medicine. After all, it was my roof that caused his problem.''

''Good girl. Matt needs a nice lady like you around.'' Pete whistled the rest of the way to the house.

After the milk was stowed in the kitchen and the pickup loaded, Pete and Jackson said their farewells. Gomez had followed along and stood beside the passenger door whining.

''I think Gomez wants to go with you,'' Eve said to Pete. ''You've certainly made a friend.''

''I wouldn't mind him coming along for a visit. Wouldn't mind a'tall. You care?'' he asked Eve.

''Not at all, but he's a digger and a real free spirit.''

Pete cackled. ''Sounds like we could be soul mates.'' He opened the door. ''Wanna come with me, boy?''

Gomez jumped in the truck without hesitation. When they drove away, the dog was sitting in the middle, and Eve could have sworn that he was smiling.

As night fell, Matt sat in the kitchen, his injured leg propped on a pillowed chair, stroking Pansy and watching Eve bustle around fixing spaghetti and salad. The smell of bread in the oven had his stomach growling. The sight of Eve bending over to tend it had another part of his anatomy growling as well.

God, she was gorgeous. Sexy. Bright. And with an independent spirit and a heart as big as Texas. Perfect. Even without a lick of makeup and with her hair mussed, she was the most fantastic woman he'd ever met. Totally unassuming. He knew exactly what it would be like to wake up with her head on the pillow next to his.

He could hardly wait.

"Are you ready?" Eve asked.

"Absolutely. Name the time."

She gave him one of those magical smiles. "I'm talking about eating our dinner. What's on your mind? Or should I ask?"

Matt winked. "Eating's good, too."

Eve served their meal, and they ate at the kitchen table surrounded by the clean, fresh smell of new paint. She was a great cook, and he devoured every morsel on his plate. Twice.

"Want some more?" she asked.

He patted his belly. "I'm full up to the gills."

"No room for ice cream? With chocolate sauce?"

"Give me an hour or two."

She shook a pill from one of the medicine bottles. "Your antibiotic. Do you need a pain pill now?"

He declined, though truthfully, now that the feeling had returned, his calf smarted a bit.

When she got up to clear the table, he rose to help as well. "Off your feet, Matt Crow. You must be careful of your leg."

"Honey, it's not that big a deal. Honest. I had lots worse injuries playing football and barely missed a quarter."

She shook her head. "Nope. I promised your grandfather that I would take care of you, and I intend to. Sit."

Charlie meowed as if to second the order.

"Yes, ma'am. Yes, sir." He grinned and sat. Pansy jumped back into his lap. Bless that wily old bird's heart. Thanks to Grandpa Pete, he had Eve all to himself for the next couple of days and nights. If he was smart, he might be able to milk it for a while longer. If Kyle didn't mess up his play house by telling her that his injury wasn't much more than a scratch.

He watched as Eve cleaned the kitchen, fantasized about the slender fingers that were now wielding a sponge across the countertop. He loved her hands, loved her long, supple fingers, and ached to have them touch him. Touch him all over.

Everywhere.

She glanced up, frowning. "I knew that I should have insisted on that pain pill. You're hurting, aren't you?"

"Hurting?"

"Yes, you groaned."

Matt tried to conceal his laughter with a coughing fit. "I'll manage for a while yet."

They sat on the porch for a long time, talking and watching the stars. Later, Eve fixed bowls of ice cream, and they talked some more. Charlotte laid her head on Matt's thigh, and he scratched behind her ears. All of Eve's animals seemed to have taken to him. Now if only their mistress would follow their lead, he'd be set.

"Are you going to feel like making the trips next week?" she asked.

"What trips?"

"The ones to check out Crow Airlines operations."

"Ohhhh, those trips." He'd forgotten all about the junket he'd planned to have her to himself for several days. "I'm sure there won't be a problem. Kyle just said a day or two's rest ought to do it."

"And speaking of rest, I think it's time you were in bed."

Her words conjured up all sorts of visions. "And you?" His voice sounded thick even to him.

"I'm going to bed, too."

They went inside, and the animals followed, scattering to their favorite places to pass the night. Eve locked the front door, then walked him to the guest room.

"Good night," she said softly, her chin lifting ever so slightly.

He took the faint action as permission to kiss her. And kiss her he did. His mouth met hers with a hunger a thousand times more potent than any craving for food.

When she sighed against his lips, his heart kicked into overdrive and his tongue plunged deeply. He groaned for real and pulled her closer against him.

"Come to bed with me," he whispered.

"I—I can't. Your leg."

"To hell with my leg. God, Eve, I want you. I ache for you."

He felt her stiffen. She shook her head. "I'm not ready for this. I may never be. Look, I'm simply not the type for casual—"

"*Casual!* I'm not after casual!"

Bowie growled; Lucy bristled; Charlie hissed; Charlotte went dead still. *"To-ré-a-dor,"* Caruso sang with gusto as Pansy and Minerva disappeared in a flash.

"Sorry," he said, lowering his volume to almost a whisper. "Sweetheart, there's nothing casual about the way I feel. I asked you once to marry me. I'm asking again. Marry me, Eve. Tonight. Tomorrow. Next week. Name the time."

"Oh, Matt, be serious. We barely know each other. And what in the world would somebody like you want with somebody like me? You're much too handsome and sophisticated for me."

"Come off it, Eve. I don't know what the hell you're talking about. I'm neither handsome nor sophisticated, and you're perfect for me. If anything, you're much too lovely. I'll probably have to carry a bull whip just to keep your admirers away. Did I tell you that I'm the jealous type?"

She laughed. "Ah, Matt Crow, you do have a way with words. If I thought you were serious…" She sighed.

"Honey, I've been trying to tell you that I *am* serious. Damned serious. The first time I saw you, I was convinced that you were an angel sent from heaven just for me, but the way you make me feel isn't very pious. You turn me on like a house afire."

Eve fought the thrill that his words sparked, wanting desperately to believe them, wanting desperately to be something she was not—glamorous, earthy, sexy. She was none of those things, and the little experience she'd had with men had proven that she was a total dud in bed. She studied her toes and gathered up gumption enough to say what had to be said.

"Look, Matt, I appreciate your attentions. I really do. You make me feel very…special, but I don't see any possibility of a long-term relationship between us. Despite what you say, I think we're totally mismatched. Plus there's the problem of our doing business together. Having affairs with clients is a terrible practice. Think how awkward things will be when your interest fizzles."

Her teeth were chattering from nervousness when he lifted her chin. "Honey—"

Her eyes darted away from his mesmerizing dark ones. "And there's the family to consider. That's even worse. It could cause all sorts of problems. I think that it's better if we're just friends." She stuck out her hand. "Deal?"

He took her outstretched hand and brought it to his lips. "I guess that I'll have to take what I can get for the moment, but I'm making no promises."

The tip of his tongue slowly circled each knuckle of her hand. Using every ounce of fortitude that she possessed, Eve pulled her hand away, turned, and walked briskly to her room.

Matt lay in bed, his hands laced behind his head. He couldn't have slept a wink if his life had depended on it. His libido was cranked up to high and giving him fits.

He wanted Eve so bad, he could taste it. Taste her sweetness mixed with ice cream and chocolate. Her smell lingered on his T-shirt and on his skin. Woman and wildflowers and yeasty bread.

She'd laughed at his proposal. Dammit, he'd asked her to marry him—twice—and she hadn't taken him seriously. Too, he was beginning to realize that she had a monumental inferiority complex and walls around her heart ten feet thick. He understood inferiority complexes; he'd had one of his own to overcome. What could he do to convince her that not only was she a beautiful, desirable woman, but that he was truly crazy about her?

The only thing he could think of was just to wear her down and scale those walls—which was exactly what he planned to do. Eve had some feelings for him; he was sure of it. She couldn't have kissed him the way she did without having some feelings.

He meant to have her. From now on, he was going to be like Chinese water torture.

The door creaked, and he glanced toward it.

Eve stood there, the hallway light surrounding her like an aura, turning her pale hair into glistening moonbeams.

"Matt," she whispered.

He sat up, about to open wide his arms.

"You forgot your medicine."

A raucous racket made Matt's eyes pop open. Caruso? No, he thought as Caruso sang out, "Figaro! Figaro! Fi-ga-ro!" from the living room. Even if Ca-

ruso insisted on singing that operatic mess, at least
the bird was on key. Matt reminded himself to teach
the myna some Waylon or Willie or at least some
Garth Brooks songs.

The racket came again.

A rooster! And, Lord, it wasn't even daylight yet.
Matt scowled into the darkness and groaned. Pansy
meowed and snuggled closer. Sometime during the
night, the cat had sneaked into his room and curled
up beside him.

His leg throbbed and was stiff. He stumbled to the
bathroom, got a glass of water and took a pill.

"Let's get some more shut-eye, girl," Matt mumbled as he climbed back in bed and pulled the covers
over his head.

Eve wanted to throttle Winston Churchill. Caruso,
too. She hoped that Matt slept through the noise. One
never knew when the rooster would decide to crow.
After she let out Minerva and the dogs, she tiptoed
to the guest room and peered through the crack
where the door was ajar. Matt was still an unmoving
bulge under the covers. She tiptoed away and went
to the kitchen.

The new ceiling and fresh paint made the room
brighter, and it looked a hundred times better. Trou-
ble was, the cabinets and the old linoleum now
looked seedy by comparison. She poured herself a
cup of coffee and stared at the cabinets.

Hmmm. If she painted just the cabinets on the bottom this morning, they would be dry by the time the
dogs came in that evening. Hmmm.

She tiptoed back to Matt's door.

He hadn't moved.

She returned to the kitchen and washed down the cabinets, poured another cup of coffee and spread newspapers from the recycling bin over the floor.

By the time Matt entered the kitchen, hair tousled and dressed in nothing but a pair of baggy warm-up pants, she was almost finished.

"What are you *doing?*" he asked. "And what time is it?"

She laughed. "It's almost eleven, and I'm painting the cabinets. You look like you could use some coffee."

"Coffee would be good. Is there some made?"

"Just brewed a fresh pot. Sit down and I'll pour a cup for you."

"Honey, I'm not an invalid. I can get my own—" Eve's stern look clipped his protest. "Yes, ma'am." He sat.

She insisted on propping his leg on a pillow and stirring his coffee. "There you go. Let me finish this last door, and I'll fix you some brunch. How about French toast and maple syrup and hash brown potatoes?"

"Sounds great. I could get used to this."

She laughed. God, he loved to hear the sound of her laughter.

"Don't get too used to it. When that gash heals, you're on your own, buster."

He felt guilty for playing on her sympathy.

But only a little guilty.

Eve had a difficult time eating. She kept staring at Matt's bare chest, fork frozen halfway to her mouth, maple syrup dripping onto her lap. She supposed that she could have asked him to put on a shirt, but she didn't want to seem so goosey. She tried to keep her attention on the French toast, but her eyes kept wandering to his pecs. Or to the darling dimple in his chin. Or to the dark beginnings of a beard. How would the rough stubble feel against the tender skin of her breast?

For the longest time, a bead of syrup at the corner of his mouth kept her entranced. She had the strangest urge to lick it off. The admission set her eyes flying to his; her face flushed with heat. He was watching her watch him.

Slowly, deliberately, the tip of his tongue eased out and slid in a maddeningly torpid path along his lower lip to the amber drop, then stroked back and forth over the spot to capture the sweetness waiting there.

She remembered how that tongue felt on her lips.

Her breasts prickled; her belly tightened; an aching throb began to pulsate low in her body. She dropped her fork with a clatter and jumped to her feet.

"Excuse me. I just remembered something I need to do in the barn. I'll be right back." She hurried from the house as if the hounds of hell were on her heels.

She'd never had such a consuming and visceral reaction to a man before. The intensity of her feelings frightened her.

This wasn't going to work, she told herself. It wasn't going to work at all. How could she spend the rest of the day and another night alone with this man without ending up in his bed?

Eight

"**I**s it butter yet?" Matt asked, looking up from his task with the churn.

"You're asking *me?* All I know about making butter is written on that sheet of paper." Eve put down her paintbrush, climbed down from the stepladder, then read the directions again.

One of Jackson's hands had arrived about one o'clock Sunday afternoon with a tall crockery churn, wooden dasher, four wooden butter presses and a sheet of notebook paper with spidery writing giving succinct instructions for the use of the items.

The batch of milk with extra cream, which Eve had left out the night before just as Pete had told her, had turned into a gloppy mess called clabber. The clabber was poured into the churn, and Matt volunteered to man the dasher while Eve painted the upper cabinets in the kitchen.

The dasher looked like a short broom handle with a wooden *X* on the end instead of straws. The handle extended through a hole in the lid of the churn, and the idea was to beat the dasher up and down through the curdled milk until butter formed. That, according to Alma Jane, was when you could "feel it ball up and see it squish through the hole when the dasher is drawn up against the lid."

"Did you feel it ball up?" Eve asked.

Matt rolled his eyes. Eve snickered.

"Okay, then, draw the dasher up slowly to the lid," she said.

"See any butter?"

"Not yet. Churn some more."

Matt groaned. "How about I buy a few pounds at the supermarket?"

"Oh, Matt. It's not the same. I want to do this for your grandfather. He said that homemade butter is twice as good as store-bought."

Fifteen minutes later, Matt said, "You know, this stuff is beginning to feel different."

Eve tapped down the top on the paint can, then washed her hands. "It's about time to check." Kneeling beside the churn, she held the lid and said, "Pull the dasher up slowly."

When soft yellow stuff squished through the hole and around the handle, Eve squealed with delight. "It's butter! I think it's butter!"

Matt dragged a bit on his finger and tasted it. He grinned. "Bedamned if it isn't."

With a little work and a lot of laughter, they managed to scoop the globs of butter from the milk and off the dasher. They transferred the butter to the presses that squeezed off the excess liquid and molded it into a pretty form with a flower on top. When they were finished, they had three whole pounds and part of another.

"These are for Pete," Eve said, pointing to the three whole ones. "But I'll make some biscuits, and we can try the extra."

"You can make biscuits?"

"Sure, but the ones I had in mind come in a can."

Matt insisted on pouring up the buttermilk left in the churn while Eve made biscuits.

Matt smeared the last buttered bite with jelly and popped it into his mouth. "Grandpa Pete was right. Homemade butter is great."

Eve smiled. "You did a good job."

He flexed the muscles in his arm and struck a Mr. Universe pose. "Champion churner."

She laughed. "Don't let it go to your head. I need to take the butter to Pete and collect Gomez. Feel up to the drive?"

"Sure. You've never seen his place, have you?"

"The Trading Post? No. But I've heard Irish describe it as a big two-story log building with everything under the sun for sale downstairs and his living quarters upstairs. And she mentioned some…very unusual tourist cabins that she stayed in."

"Very unusual—if you consider stucco wigwams painted in loud colors unusual. That's the place. How about I drive?"

"Nope. Your leg is injured, remember?"

"Oh, yeah." He looped his arm around her shoulders and leaned against her as he hobbled from the kitchen.

Eve lifted an eyebrow. "I thought it was your other leg."

He did a fast shuffle and began limping on the other leg. "Referred pain."

She studied his dark eyes, but they reflected total innocence. *Innocence*, hah! But, dear Lord, he had beautiful eyes. Sexy, soulful. Bedroom eyes. Eyes that made her want to— *Stop it!* she told herself and looked away before her thoughts went totally X-rated.

When the thumb of his dangling hand casually brushed her nipple, she glanced quickly at his eyes again. They held the same practiced innocence. Very practiced.

"Cut it out," she snapped.

"Cut what out, honey?"

"You know perfectly well what, and I'd prefer that you not call me 'honey.'"

The same thumb again brushed her nipple. She stiffened. "Don't tell me that was an accident, Matt Crow."

"I wouldn't dream of it." His thumb made a slow circle, then his fingers slid beneath her breast to cup it in his palm. "Rather, I did dream of it. All night I dreamt of touching you there." He turned her toward him. "And kissing you again. Here." He tipped her chin and pressed his lips against her throat.

Eve almost melted into a mindless puddle.

"How does that feel, darlin'?" he murmured against her skin.

"Heavenly."

"Shall I stop?"

"Not just yet." His tongue moved higher, and his hands moved lower. She groaned. "In a minute you'll have to stop. But not just yet."

"You like that?"

"What's not to like?"

Their lips met urgently. Their breathing was hot and heavy. The dogs began to bark. Minerva squealed. Caruso sang, *"Sempre, sempre libera..."* in a glass-shattering soprano. A car door slammed.

Eve startled and pushed away. Matt moaned in protest and tried to gather her back into his arms.

She struggled. "Matt, someone's coming."

"Tell them to go away." He reached for her again.

"Anybody home?" a familiar male voice called. A knock rattled the screen door.

"Eve?" a female voice chimed in. "Yoo-hoo."

Eve swatted Matt's busy hands. "Stop it," she whispered. "Come on in," she called to Irish and Kyle.

"Damn," Matt muttered, moving away.

Eve gathered a smattering of composure, plastered a smile on her face and went to greet her sister and brother-in-law. Matt grumbled along behind.

"Hi, you two. What brings you out?"

"We were on our way to an antique shop down the way when the bottom fell out of the sky," Irish said. "We decided to stop by until it let up a bit." She shook the big red-and-white umbrella she carried and leaned it against a porch chair.

"Oh, is it raining?" Eve asked, peering out the door.

"Pouring. Don't tell me you hadn't noticed."

"Darn. We were going to Pete's to take him some fresh butter."

"*Butter?*" Kyle asked.

Eve nodded. "Matt and I made it."

"*Matt?*"

"Darling, you sound like a parrot," Irish said, brushing by her husband. "Eve, have you been painting?"

"Yes. I've almost finished the kitchen cabinets. Can you smell it?"

"Mmmm. Plus you have a smear on your cheek." Irish smiled knowingly. "Matt seems to have a matching one."

Eve felt her face go hot, and she swiped at her cheek with her shirtsleeve. "Would you like some coffee? I'll go make some coffee. Matt, perhaps Kyle could look at your leg while he's here. He seems to be in a great deal of pain, Kyle."

"Pain, huh? Sure, I'll look at it. And coffee would be great. Drop your britches, Matt."

"Dammit, Kyle!" Matt roared.

"Boys!" Laughing, Irish herded Eve toward the kitchen. "Let's make the coffee, Sis, and you can show me your handiwork. How did you like the color I selected for the cabinets?"

Eve started coffee and put another pan of biscuits in the oven while Irish admired the cabinets that were almost finished. Eve explained her plans to paint soft designs on the door fronts, and they discussed possibilities for curtains and a new floor.

Because of the differences in age, Eve and Irish had never been friends. Eve was always the grubby baby sister, then Irish was off to New York and they seldom spent time together. Now, as adults, the sisters were able to talk in a way that they never had before. Eve loved the new closeness they had found. How very, very lucky she was that Fate had brought her this wonderful job in Texas.

Life was just about perfect.

Kyle inspected the place he'd stitched. "Looks fine to me. A neat piece of work, if I do say so myself. No sign of infection. A great deal of pain, Eve said? I don't understand why."

"Well…I wouldn't exactly say that I'm in serious pain. Not from my leg anyway." Matt grinned. "Let's just say that I enjoy Eve's brand of TLC, and I need an excuse to hang around for a while."

"Why you dirty, rotten scoundrel," Kyle said, grinning. "Sounds like I need to ask your intentions toward my young sister-in-law."

"She's not that young, and my intentions are strictly honorable. I'm crazy about her, Kyle. I have been since I first laid eyes on her at your wedding."

"And how does she feel about you?"

Matt shrugged. "We're working on it. Rather, I'm working on it. She doesn't seem to take me seriously, and I just need a few reasons to spend some more time with her."

"Like your poor, lame leg?"

Matt chuckled. "Yeah. Like that."

Kyle frowned. "Cuz, I heard Eve mention that she's in charge of the Crow Airlines account at the ad agency. Seems like a handy coincidence."

"Uh-huh."

"You didn't by any chance arrange for Eve to get that job, did you, buddy?"

"Who? Me?"

Kyle swiped his face with his hand. "Oh, boy."

"What?"

"Damn. You did, didn't you?"

Matt didn't respond, but his expression must have given him away because Kyle gave him a blistering lecture. "For a lot of reasons I won't go into, Eve's very sensitive about making it on her own. And neither she nor Irish like being deceived about anything. I almost lost Irish by pulling something stupid like that. If you want my advice, you'd better come clean right away."

"Think I ought to tell her that my leg is okay, huh?"

"I'm not just talking about your leg, Matt."

"Kyle, do me a favor, please. Don't mention our talk to Irish or Eve. If nothing else, consider it doctor-client privilege."

"I keep forgetting that you trained to be a lawyer. I won't say anything, but trust me when I tell you that if you continue to deceive Eve, it's eventually gonna come back and bite you on the butt."

Nine

Sam Marcus stuck his head in the door. "Hey, boss, a fellow is here to pick you up. Want me to load your bags?"

Eve glanced up from the radio spot she was reading. "Thanks, Sam. Tell him that I'll be right there. Just let me finish this."

Bryan had been late again with his copy. Sometimes she wondered if he stayed up late nights, thinking of ways to complicate her life. No, she didn't need Bryan Belo to do that. She'd managed to complicate it enough herself. She must have read at least a half-dozen articles on the imprudence of becoming romantically involved with clients. It could be the professional equivalent of shooting oneself in the foot, but had she listened to that little voice in her brain telling her, *No!*?

Of course not.

She'd managed to stay out of bed with Matt—but just barely. She'd tried to explain to him between bone-melting kisses that a relationship between them wasn't wise, but he didn't seem to get it. Monday morning had been a relief of sorts—she could escape close confinement with him. He'd gone to his grandfather's with the butter, and she'd gone to work.

She hadn't seen him in the two days since they'd parted at her front gate. He had called, but she'd tried to keep their conversations brief and businesslike, mostly making the arrangements for their Crow Airlines junket. She'd declined invitations to lunch, dinner, a musical show and a baseball game.

And, darn it, she missed him.

With only the tiniest push, she could really fall for a man like Matt. No, not a man like Matt. Matt. He was one of a kind. And when she thought of the way he kissed her and held her and whispered—

"Earth to Eve. Earth to Eve."

Startled, Eve looked up to find Nancy in front of her desk. "Sorry. I was daydreaming." She hurriedly began gathering her briefcase and her purse.

"Hon, if I was flying off into the wild blue yonder for five fun-filled days and four glorious nights with that hunk, I'd be daydreaming, too." Nancy sighed. "He is some good-looking man. And nice, too. Did you know that he has been voted one of Dallas's ten most eligible bachelors for the past five years or so? I've even seen photos in the *Morning News* of him escorting movie stars to some of the disease balls."

Nancy's words were like a stake through Eve's

heart, but she covered the pain by casually asking, "What's a disease ball?"

"The big, formal charity bashes for diabetes or CF or heart disease or some such. I always figured that the cost of the parties would fund research for a year, but I guess the 'money folks' need to have an occasion to open their pockets. I understand that Matt and his family are always very generous with their donations. I think he's the honorary chairman of Big Brothers or something."

"Is he? I haven't heard him say." She handed Bryan's radio spot to Nancy. "This is great. Tell Pat to get it started right away. Candy has my itinerary. I told Jimmy, the boy who's caring for the animals, to call you if he needs to get in touch with me. I'll be checking in with you tomorrow, but call me if you need anything."

"Everything is under control," Nancy said. "Come on, I'll walk you to the door."

Flotillas of buzzing bees rode the great swells that roiled in her stomach. On the one hand, she was excited about spending the next few days flying around the state with Matt; on the other, she was filled with monumental dread.

She rose, straightened the jacket of her gray suit, and marched down the hall.

"Smile," Nancy said. "You act like you're going to your beheading."

Eve managed a chuckle. "I may be. Keep your fingers crossed that this goes okay. I'd hate to lose this account for us."

"Not a chance. I think our Mr. Crow has the hots for you. Go for it, babe."

"Bite your tongue, Nancy."

Nancy only laughed.

A tall, sandy-haired man in a dark western suit stood by the front door, his white Stetson in his hand. "Miss Ellison?"

"Eve Ellison. That's me."

"I'm Billy Don Durham," he said with a gap-toothed smile. He opened the door. "Right this way, ma'am. I'm driving you to Love."

Eve felt the blood leave her face. "You're *what?*"

"Driving you to Love. Crow flies out of Love Field instead of the big Dallas-Ft. Worth airport. Shoot, it's no more than five or ten minutes from here this time of day. That's one of the things folks like about flying Crow. Besides being friendly and fun and having the number one safety record in the industry, it's convenient."

Eve recovered quickly…well, fairly quickly. Nancy was giggling, so her thoughts must have been noticeable—at least to Nancy. "That's wonderful, Billy Don. I didn't realize there was another airport so close to the city. Nancy, make a note of that. We need to capitalize on the convenience issue in the campaign."

"Will do," Nancy managed to say with a straight face.

"Right this way, ma'am," the cowboy chauffeur said.

Matt had offered to pick her up himself, but she had declined, saying that she wanted an introduction to the airline without being in the company of the boss. They had finally compromised with his sending a driver in an ordinary car.

The car waiting at the curb was a blue Buick with a ding in the rear fender.

After a very short ride to the smaller airport—which was still considerably larger than the main facility of many cities—Billy Don pulled to a stop. The employees of Crow Airlines were immediately recognizable. They wore jeans, white western shirts with a black crow on the pocket and black cowboy hats with a black feather in the band. Every one of them wore a big smile.

"Mornin', ma'am," a man said to her as he checked in her bags. "Glad you're going as the Crow flies. Where you headed today?"

"Houston," she said, handing him her ticket.

"I'll see that your bags get there." His smile broadened as he tipped his hat and returned her ticket with her claim checks. "Follow that yellow line inside the door to Gate 5. Have a good day."

"Thanks." Eve felt herself smiling as she followed the yellow line to the gate.

As she neared the area, she could hear country music and someone singing about "friends in low places."

At the check-in counter, a woman, who was dressed in a fringed blue-and-white shirt and a blue cowboy hat with the familiar black feather in the band, greeted her with another smile. "Good mornin'. Glad you're flying Crow today. Hear the weather is great in Houston. Our flight time will be about forty-five minutes." She handed Eve a red plastic card. "This is your boarding pass. Listen for the red cattle call and go along with the herd. Take any seat that's available, just promise that you won't sit in a stranger's lap.'' The woman laughed and winked.

Eve grinned. "I'll promise. You don't have reserved seating?''

"Nope. We just load 'em up and move 'em out. We get you there safe, cheap, on time—and we make you like it. Also, if you'd like a cup of coffee, help yourself over there by the windows. We don't serve coffee in the air—just juice, water and soft drinks.''

"Fair enough.'' She looked around for Matt but didn't see him, so she found a seat in the area and began reading a book she'd brought along, her toes tapping to the rhythm of the taped music.

In a few minutes, a young blonde in jeans, a red-and-white fringed shirt and a red cowboy hat stuck her fingers in her mouth and whistled. "Hey, all you red folks, let's go to Houston! Follow me.''

Eve and about a quarter of the people waiting rose and followed the waving red hat to board the plane. Matt still wasn't anywhere to be seen. She considered waiting, then decided not. After all, she'd wanted an authentic experience.

Other friendly personnel in cowboy hats greeted the passengers at the entrance to the plane. "Grab you a good place quick,'' a petite redhead in a blue hat said. "The next bunch is hot on your heels. We're rolling in ten minutes. If you're carrying a bunch of hand luggage, you have to move to the back to stow it and take your chances on a prime seat.''

The other passengers seemed familiar with the drill, for they moved briskly down the aisles and took places.

Eve spotted Matt sitting in the third row. A black cowboy hat was in the seat next to him.

He grinned as she approached. "May I offer you this place, ma'am?" He moved his hat.

"Why, thank you, sir. How very kind of you."

As soon as she was settled, he asked, "What do you think so far?"

"Great. Can we really be rolling in ten minutes?"

Matt glanced at his watch. "Seven and a half now. You can bet that Billy Don will be taxiing to the runway on the dot. My folks know their business."

"Billy Don? Is he—?"

"Captain Billy Don Durham. He's the best pilot around. All my people are top-notch."

"You had the *pilot* pick me up?"

Matt shrugged. "He's happily married with two kids, has an excellent safety record, and it was on his way." A grin slid across his face. "Besides, Billy Don and I go way back. I trust him."

Just as Matt had predicted, at departure time every passenger was seated and the attendants were giving the safety instructions as the plane began to taxi toward the runway. "Buckle up, folks. Here we go." With a "yee-ha!" they were airborne.

As soon as the plane had leveled off a bit, the red-haired hostess started down the aisle juggling foil packets high in the air, laughing and stopping to toss the complimentary sunflower seeds as she went, then grabbing a new supply from the bulging pocket of her apron. "Here you go, pardner," she said as she lobbed the packs. "Laura's coming along with something to wet your whistle."

Laura, the blonde in the red hat, wore a vendor's

tray and dispensed small bottled drinks. "I have cold orange juice, apple juice and Texas spring water, folks. Rusty will be back with the soft drinks in a shake."

Matt took orange juice and Eve opted for apple. "Why don't you have the usual carts with drinks?" Eve asked. "And I notice you don't serve alcohol, either. Why?"

"Couple of reasons. Time and money. All our flights are short, and there are bars in the airports. Economically, it makes sense. We don't need extra personnel to serve, nor do we need ice, glasses, coffee cream, or all the other stuff that has to be contracted out. I figure that our customers had rather we keep fares low and put the extra money into topnotch maintenance crews—which we do."

"Makes sense. I'm impressed."

"This is Captain Billy Don Durham," a voice drawled from the intercom. "We're on our way to Houston—unless anybody needs to stop off at Tyler for something. No? Well then, I'm gonna put my spurs to old paint, and the good Lord willin' and the Creek don't rise, we'll be pulling up to the gate at Hobby Airport in twenty-two minutes. Looks like it's warm and muggy in Houston today.

"Out the window on your left is the Trinity River. If you look real fast, you might see Zeke Tatum fishing. Oops, too late. And over on your right is Russ McIver's hog farm. Coming up is the Davy Crockett National Forest. Keep an eye out for the big bunch of trees. Thanks for flying Crow Airlines today, and if we can do something special for you, just give a holler. We aim to please."

Eve laughed. "Are all the pilots so folksy?"

"Some are, some aren't. But we like a certain attitude at Crow. Safety is always first, and we like being on time, but otherwise, we don't take ourselves too seriously."

"Anybody hanker for some more sunflower seeds?" perky Laura asked. "We have a few left." When a couple of hands went up, she lobbed one to a young man and tossed another behind her.

It seemed that the trip had hardly begun when a bell dinged and the attendants said, "Buckle up, buckaroos."

Billy Don landed without a bobble, and in no time they were off the plane and waiting at the luggage carousel.

Eve pointed out her garment bag and other small case, which Matt snagged along with his two pieces.

"This all you brought?" Matt asked.

She nodded. "That's it."

Irish had helped her pack, or she would have probably brought half a dozen pieces. Eve had never done much traveling, and she certainly didn't know what to bring along for their jaunt. With Irish's supervision and a couple of packable dresses from the former model's own wardrobe, Eve was now perfectly mix-and-match color-coordinated. Irish had even included written instructions for what to wear when and with what. Amazingly, Eve ended up with something for every occasion that fit into two pieces of luggage.

She'd been very confident that all contingencies were covered until she saw Matt frowning at her bags. Suddenly her old insecurities started scratching at her insides. "Is something wrong?" she asked him.

He smiled. "Not at all. I just didn't think women could pack for nearly a week and bring less than a pickup load of stuff." He motioned for a skycap who loaded their things onto a cart. "This way to the helicopter."

Eve's eyes widened. "The helicopter?"

By the time the bellman had escorted them to a huge suite atop the Galleria area hotel, Matt knew he'd made a serious mistake. He'd meant to delight Eve with the fancy helicopter, the limo, the luxurious rooms. He'd planned to wine her and dine her in Houston's finest, and sweep her off her feet.

Problem was, she looked miserable. And she acted as jumpy as a long-tailed cat in a roomful of rocking chairs.

"Well, what do you think of the place?" he asked, gesturing around the suite that was filled with French antiques, lots of marble, and enormous bouquets of fresh flowers.

Her pretty blue eyes darted around as if the Texas chain-saw murderer might jump out of a closet at any minute. "It's very…grand, isn't it? And large. Very large. I think I hear an echo." He watched her swallow as if something were stuck in her throat, and eye the grand piano and the carved gold chairs.

"You don't like it here." Matt felt thoroughly disgusted with himself. He'd tried to play big dog and screwed up big-time. He hadn't remembered that Eve was different from most of the women he'd dated in the past. She wasn't interested in seeing and being seen, in fancy hotels or diamonds or furs—except the kind of fur that was attached to live four-legged critters who barked or meowed or brayed. That was one of the things that was so endearing about her. One of the many things.

He prayed that he hadn't done irreparable harm to their relationship.

"It's…fine. Very…nice. I need to hang up my things. You mentioned something about lunch. What are the plans?"

Actually, his plans were to take her to one of the posh places nearby, but he quickly revised his plans. "Did you bring along any jeans?"

She nodded.

"Let's change, and I'll surprise you."

She nodded again and started for her room, shoulders slumped and still perusing the place with that godawful overwhelmed expression. Matt wanted to drop-kick himself from Houston to Oklahoma City. He didn't have a clue as to where they were going for lunch, but he was going to do a fast shuffle and come up with something that she would love.

Ten

Lunch was at a little place a few blocks away that the concierge recommended. They sat on mismatched chairs at scarred tables and ate lentil soup and thick goat-cheese-and-sprout sandwiches on whole grain bread. Instead of wine, they drank iced herbal tea. For dessert, apple crisp with raisins and crunchy bran topping was served with creamy sauce. Except for the raisins, which he pushed to the side of his bowl, Matt had to admit that the whole meal was damned good. The smile that Eve bestowed on him was even better.

"Enjoy your lunch?" he asked.

"It was fabulous. I'm stuffed."

"I hope you saved some room for popcorn and cotton candy."

She frowned, then looked pensive. "Where are we going?"

"You'll see."

Matt paid the check, and they left.

A few minutes later, as their rented sedan rounded a curve in the freeway, Eve said, "That looks like the Astrodome."

"That's because it *is* the Astrodome. It's grown outdated now, but in its heyday, it was like the eighth wonder of the world. It's still something, isn't it?"

"I'll say. Is that where we're going?"

"Not today—that is, unless you want to. I thought that after we got settled in our new digs, we'd go to AstroWorld and ride the Texas Cyclone. It's the mother of all Texas roller coasters. You game?"

"I'd love to," she said, looking as excited as a kid. "I *adore* roller coasters. How did you know?"

He shrugged and tried to hide a grin. "Lucky guess." That and a quick call to Irish. "AstroWorld has ten or eleven roller coasters. We'll ride all of them."

And they did.

Every one of them.

By the time Matt climbed off the Ultra Twister, his stomach was a sorry mess. Eve seemed in her element. She was laughing and her eyes shone brightly.

"Oh, this place is wonderful!" she exclaimed, tucking her arm through his.

"Glad you like it. There's a Six Flags in Dallas, you know, and a Fiesta Texas in San Antonio. They have roller coasters, too."

"Really? That gives me a great idea for an ad campaign. You can offer a roller coaster tour—or other Texas tours based on the major attractions of different cities. That would bring in a larger market of tourists for Crow."

"Sounds great," Matt said. "Ready to go back to the hotel?"

"Could we ride Thunder River first?"

Soaking wet from the river ride and still laughing, Matt and Eve rode the elevator up to their suite at the new hotel nearby. She couldn't remember when she'd enjoyed an afternoon so much or laughed so hard.

Matt unlocked and swung open the door. While their accommodations were very nice indeed, the more modest chain's suite was a far cry from the museum at the Galleria. At least she wasn't terrified that she would drip on an antique here.

As soon as the door closed, Matt took her in his arms. "Have fun?"

"Loads." She brushed a drop of water from his chin. "You're wet."

He licked a drop from her nose. "So are you."

"I think we ought to take a shower."

He grinned. "I'm game. My shower or yours?"

"Both. Separately." She laughed and pushed away. "Where are we going for dinner? How shall I dress?"

"Well, I—" He looked very uncomfortable. "Where would you like to go?"

"Do you have reservations somewhere fancy?"

"Well, I thought we might go to Café Annie's, but I'd just as soon go to Luby's Cafeteria if that's what you would like. They both have great food."

Matt was such a dear that she wanted to hug him all over again. He'd obviously planned to take her to the posh place with a string of stars in its rating. Even though she'd honestly rather change into dry jeans and go to the cafeteria for macaroni and cheese, she couldn't bear to disappoint him. And perhaps it was time she began to broaden her experience. Irish was always telling her that she was in a rut.

"Oh, I've read about Café Annie's. I'd love to go there." And the truth was, even though she was a little nervous about going to the spot where the elite dined, she was also a little excited about wearing the dress that Irish insisted she borrow. Irish had sworn that Eve looked dazzling in it, but after all, Irish was her sister and a very kind person.

"You sure?"

She nodded. "If you don't think that I'll embarrass you."

"Embarrass me? Are you crazy, woman? Why on earth do you think that you would embarrass me?"

"Well, I'm not…in the same league with the kind of women who go there, the kind that you usually…whatever." Feeling foolish, she lowered her eyes and bit her lip.

He lifted her chin. "And what kind of women do you think that I usually…whatever?"

She couldn't meet his eyes. "Oh, beautiful, self-assured…sexy."

"Dammit, Eve, what does it take to convince you?" He took her hand and pulled her over to a large mirror. "Look," he demanded, stepping behind her. "Look at yourself. Take a good look. What do you see?"

What she saw was a mess. Her shirt was damp and wilted; her lipstick was long gone; her hair went every which way. "A wreck."

His arms circled her waist and his eyes met hers in the mirror. "Want to know what I see?"

"I—I'm not sure."

"I see the face of an angel with big, beautiful eyes the color of a summer sky that flash like blue diamonds when you get excited. I see a mouth that is lush and sultry, warms me all over when it laughs and keeps me awake nights because I want to kiss it. I see hair like strands of moonbeams, and I especially like it when it's a little mussed like it is now. I see a woman just my size with a dynamite body and legs that just won't quit."

She tried to speak, but she couldn't say a word. Her eyes stayed locked with his as he brought her hand to his mouth. "And your hands," he said. "I love your hands with their long fingers. I love the way they move, the way they pat an old mule or stroke a cat or touch me."

His tongue traced a path down her thumb and around the curve to the tip of her index finger. It was a good thing that he was holding her around the waist because her knees gave.

He nuzzled the side of her neck. "I find you stunningly beautiful." He nipped her earlobe. "And very, very sexy."

Eve closed her eyes and let his words bathe her with their sweet essence. They sparked a glow deep within her that grew until her skin tingled with its warmth and her lips parted in a smile. She wanted desperately to be beautiful—for Matt.

"Give me forty-five minutes," she said in a voice that sounded too sultry for hers.

Matt strutted like a peacock through one of Houston's finest restaurants. With Eve on his arm, he felt ten feet tall. He wanted to beat his chest and let out a Tarzan yell. He wanted to smugly proclaim, "She's *mine!*"

Eve Ellison was the most ravishing thing he'd ever seen. Well, she was always beautiful, but tonight she was especially so. She wore what he'd heard women call a little black dress, but the little black dress she had on was dynamite. It clung in all the right places and showed off a pair of long legs that left him breathless.

With her pale blond hair caught back in glittery clips and hanging loose down her back, she was a stunner. He could feel the eyes of most of the men in the room—and a good number of the women's as well—on her. And every pair of those eyes was green.

"Have I told you how gorgeous you look?" Matt asked.

She laughed and her eyes sparkled with delight. "About a dozen times. I'm almost beginning to believe it."

"Believe it. I wouldn't trade you for any ten of the women here."

She seemed to glow, and she walked with a self-assured stride as they headed for a quiet table to one side, out of the flow of the see-and-be-seen crowd. Matt had spotted several business acquaintances as well as a couple of other people he knew. He'd merely nodded and did nothing to invite further communication. His total focus was on Eve. Which wasn't hard.

"Would you like a drink?" he asked her.

"Wine, I think. A white zinfandel."

"Want to try a Texas label?"

"You make wine in Texas, too?"

"You bet your boots, darlin'. Good wine. It's won a passel of awards." He ordered a bottle from a Bryan winery. "I think you'll like the food here, too. I called earlier and found out that they have several vegetarian entrees."

"You're a sweetheart."

When she smiled and touched his hand, Matt wanted to stand on the table and crow like Winston Churchill. Instead he laughed, winked, and said, "That I am. And don't you forget it."

Dinner was fabulous. And the wine pure ambrosia.

Eve kept trying to discuss campaign ideas with Matt, but he would put her off with another glass of wine or another entertaining story. His gaze whispered that he could eat her with a spoon as easily as he could devour the créme brûlée. With those sin-dark eyes on her, caressing her skin as they slid over her face, her neck, her shoulders, it was very difficult to think about business.

Actually, she thought a lot about his lips.

About how warm and soft they would feel against hers. How wet they could make her neck. Or her breasts.

Her tongue slid along the arc of her wineglass, and

she found herself wishing that it was his lips she was tracing.

She thought about his hands, about his long fingers. About all the places he could touch.

Eve thought about her hands, about all the places she wanted to touch. As their gazes met and held, the air between them was so electrified that the flowers in the table vase almost ignited.

She cupped the bowl of her glass in both hands, traced the rim with the tip of her tongue, and her toes rubbed upward along his calf.

Suddenly, he slapped his napkin on the table and stood. "Let's get out of here."

"But we don't have the check yet."

He pulled a money clip from his pocket, peeled several large bills from the bunch and slapped them on the table. "That ought to cover it."

Matt grabbed her little silk purse, took her elbow, and herded her toward the door as rapidly as if someone had yelled, "Fire!" She had to almost run to keep up.

"Where are we going in such a hurry?" she asked as he guided her outside.

"Here," he said, pushing her into a spot in the shadows.

Then he kissed her.

He kissed her with a soul-robbing intensity that curled her toes and blistered her lips. She moaned and kissed him back with equal intensity.

He went wild. His hands were everywhere. His mouth was everywhere else. Her knees began to tremble.

Matt groaned and pulled away. "This isn't going

to work. Come on.'' He grabbed her hand, and they ran for the car.

It was a miracle that Matt wasn't arrested for speeding on the way back to the hotel. It was another miracle that they weren't arrested for...other things as they rode the elevator up to their suite.

By the time they reached the door, Eve's dress was unzipped, her bra was unhooked, and Matt's jacket was hanging by one arm. His belt buckle was undone, and his tie was looped over a lamp somewhere along the route.

Barely was the door closed when, between hot kisses, clothes started flying every which way. They didn't even make it to the bedroom. Or to the couch. Matt sat her on the dining table and drove into her.

She wrapped her legs around him and cried out his name as she moved against him with all the fury of the Texas Cyclone.

It was hot and frenzied and fast.

The climax hit her with the suddenness of an eighty-degree drop on a roller coaster, and she arched her back and let the waves of pleasure roll over her, calling Matt's name again and again.

He whispered love words in her ear as the spasms went on and on, and his words made her pleasure even sweeter. Then he thrust again and joined her in exquisite gratification.

As Eve lay back with Matt beside her, their bodies were as wet from lovemaking as they'd been after Thunder River, their breath as ragged as if they'd run a marathon. Still, he covered her breast with small licks and kisses, then laid his head upon it.

"I love the way you taste," he said. "I love everything about you. Eve, I love you so."

Her heart almost stopped. *Love?* He loved her? Surely this was pillow talk. She squirmed.

His head shot up. "What's wrong?"

She laughed. "We're on the dining table, and it's becoming very hard."

Matt let out an expletive. "Honey, I'm sorry. Hell, I can't believe that I was such a horny fool that I threw you on a table. I wanted our first time to be special, gentle, romantic." He looked thoroughly disgusted with himself.

Her heart melted and she cupped his face in her hand. "Shhh. It was wonderful."

His expression softened. "It was wonderful, wasn't it? But next time I'll go slowly. I want to see and smell and taste every inch of you. I want to make it last a long, long time. Come."

Matt led her into her bedroom and their remaining bits of clothing were shed. Slowly he pulled the clips from her hair. He ran his hands through the strands and sifted the length through his fingers. He kissed her eyes, her nose, the corners of her mouth, all the time whispering sweet, sweet love words and praising each feature as he went.

His tongue traced the curve of her jaw and the shell of her ear and the line of her throat. He laid her on the bed and cupped one breast while he brushed his cheek against her nipple as it went hard. Then he licked it and blew on it. She gasped from the erotic sensation. She gasped again when his lips closed around the tip and sucked.

Eve could feel the terrible, wonderful hunger for

him building again. "Oh, Matt, what are we doing?" she whispered.

He looked up from the activity that seemed to totally engross him and smiled. It was the delightful, boyishly sexy smile, the one that melted her heart. "I thought that was obvious."

His mouth moved to her other breast. The sensation was exquisite. "I mean...I mean—we shouldn't be doing this."

"We shouldn't?" His mouth moved lower, and his tongue dipped into her navel.

"No. This isn't...wise. Ours should be a—oh, oh—a business relationship."

"Mmmmm. Shall I stop?"

She sucked in a strangled gasp and grabbed handfuls of his hair. "Not...yet. It...feels...too...good."

"Don't worry, love. I intend to take a long, long time and love you very, very thoroughly and make you feel very, very good."

He did, and it did.

Matt would have been content to spend the entire day in Eve's bed, but she convinced him that this was a business trip, and he reluctantly rose and dressed.

She gathered dozens of brochures advertising the various activities available to tourists visiting Houston and talked to some of the hotel personnel about the most popular attractions. Finally, she announced, "I think we should see NASA."

"*NASA?*"

"Yep. It's very popular with tourists, and after all, that's the new market you want to tap, isn't it?"

At that moment, he didn't give a tinker's damn about tourists. All he cared about was Eve. The trip had been planned so that they could spend time together, so that he could court her in style, convince her that she had to marry him. But God forbid if she had any inkling of his motivations. So he said, "Good point. NASA it is. And when we're finished there, we'll drive on down to Galveston. It's not far, and tourists love it. Did you bring a bathing suit?"

"Oh, no. It didn't occur to me."

"No matter. We'll buy you one there." He wiggled his eyebrows in a comic licentious expression. "Sugar, watching you model bathing suits will be pure pleasure."

Deciding to play vagabond, they tossed their luggage in the trunk and headed south on the Gulf Freeway. They spent the morning touring the space facility and museum. Matt hadn't been there before and both of them enjoyed the excursion.

Galveston was only a half hour or so from NASA, and as they drove, their nearness to the coast became apparent as the terrain became flatter and more marshy until they reached the bay and the long causeway to the island.

Matt hadn't been to Galveston in years, but Eve refreshed his memory by reading to him from more brochures she'd picked up when they'd stopped for gas.

"Oh, look at all the wonderful old houses," she exclaimed as they drove down Broadway, the boulevard that led to the Gulf. "I think some of them are open for tours."

"Want to see them?"

"Could we?"

"You betcha. Let's find a hotel along the seawall, and we'll check out the schedule."

"A hotel? But aren't we supposed to fly to San Antonio this afternoon?"

"I called my assistant before we left and told her that our plans have changed. We'll wait and go in the morning. I told her that I'd rather see you in a bathing suit."

"You didn't!" She laughed in spite of her effort to be irked with him. "You dog! What must she think?"

"Emily has three sons and a grandson. She's a hip lady." While they waited at a red light, Matt punched in a number on his cell phone. "Hey, Auntie Em, we were just talking about you. Did you make reservations for Galveston? Great…got it. We'll probably fly to San Antonio sometime in the morning. How about eleven? Great…I'll let you know. Tell Tanker to handle the Japanese thing according to his best judgment. Talk to you later, babe."

"*Babe?* You call your assistant 'babe?'"

"Sure. Either that or Auntie Em. Sometimes I call her 'sweet-patootie.' She loves it."

"Why, Matthew Crow, I'm shocked. You're a male chauvinist pig. And that's sexual harassment."

"Nope. That's affection. She *is* my Auntie Em, my dad's younger sister, and her husband and half the family call her 'sweet-patootie.'"

Eve felt like a fool and apologized for jumping to conclusions. She thought she had finally found a chink in Matt's armor, a flaw in his character. She was wrong. Matt was just about perfect.

Eleven

"Hmmm," Matt said. "Turn around again." When Eve complied, he studied her closely. "I can't decide if I like this one best or the blue one. Why don't we just take them both?"

"And the cover-ups, too?" the saleslady in the boutique asked hopefully.

"Oh, absolutely," he told her. When Eve tried to protest, he waved off her arguments. "This is a business expense. I'll write it off as research."

"Don't you think that's reaching a bit?"

He laughed. "I'll let the accounting department worry about that."

Eve knew he was teasing, but she didn't argue anymore. She was discovering that when Matt turned on that boyish charm, it was hard to say no to him about anything—not that she wanted to say no to him about much. And besides, the suits made her feel glamorous and sexy.

Or was it Matt who made her feel that way?

After they left the little shop, they did some more sightseeing and ended up at the Rainforest Pyramid, a huge glass pyramid that covered an acre and depicted the major rain forests.

"Fascinating. Positively fascinating," Eve said as they wandered through the pyramid with its exotic plants and simulated waterfalls.

Matt loved watching her. He reveled in her delight at the birds flying free in the jungle-like settings. When a large, brightly colored butterfly landed on her arm, she grew stone still as she observed it. Such a look of awe came over her face that he was totally captivated by the beauty of woman and the exotic winged creature. He wished for a camera to capture the magic of the moment.

Another butterfly, then another, then a third drifted to rest in her hair like wondrous fluttering flowers of blue and red and orange and yellow. His breath caught. Love for Eve swelled within him until he thought his chest might burst open from the power of the emotion.

There was something undefinable about this woman that drew him to her along with butterflies and stray animals, a beauty of spirit as well as body that pulled him like a magnet, captivated him, called to his core.

"Marry me," he whispered.

She laughed and the butterflies flitted away. "Stop

being so silly, Matt. What on earth would you do if I said yes?''

"I would be the happiest man in Texas. In the world. What will it take to convince you that I'm serious?''

"Time. Matt—''

A pair of giggling children ran by and the little boy fell just past them. He began to wail, and Eve knelt to help him up and comfort him. Only his pride was hurt, and by the time the child's mother arrived, Eve had the boy and girl calm, smiling, and watching the birds.

After the children and their mother walked on, Eve looped her arm through Matt's. "I wonder how Caruso is doing? Sometimes he gets neurotic if I'm gone very long.''

"*Gets* neurotic?'' Matt chuckled. "That bird is a nut case already. Why else would he pick out all his feathers?''

"The vet thinks it's allergies.'' She grinned. "Or a neurosis.''

"See?''

She laughed and laid her head on his shoulder. She couldn't recall ever in her life feeling so fantastic.

After the rain forest, they visited the beach. As they walked down the seawall steps to the sand, Eve shaded her eyes and looked out over the water. "Why isn't anybody swimming? It's a glorious day.''

Matt scanned the gentle waves lapping the shore, then checked further out. "Oh, I see what the problem is." He pointed to the swells. "See those clear-looking blobs floating on top of the water? Those are jellyfish. They appear to be innocent things floating along like big bubbles, but they have tentacles hanging down that can deal a lot of misery. If one of those devils pops you or wraps a tentacle around an arm or leg, you feel like you're on fire."

"Sounds like you've had personal experience."

"I have. When we were kids, Jackson and I both got stung pretty badly—Jackson worse than me. We ended up in the emergency room and had to cut our vacation short."

"I think I'll stay out of the water. Are they always this bad?"

Matt shook his head. "Only occasionally. I'm not sure why." He stripped off his polo shirt and tossed it atop the towels they'd brought along. "Want me to put some lotion on you? I wouldn't want you to burn that lovely skin."

"Good idea." She straightened the towels and stretched out on her tummy.

As Matt slowly stroked sunblock over her legs and back, Eve recalled the night before and all the intimate places he had stroked then. His hands were magic; his mouth was magic. Making love with him had awakened a whole new facet of her womanhood. She would never be the same again.

How could she give this up?

She didn't like to think about it.

When she was completely covered with lotion, he capped the bottle and lay down beside her.

"What about you?" she asked. "Don't you need

sunscreen?''

''Naw. It's late in the day, and besides, I never burn.''

Matt muttered a curse into the pillow he gripped as Eve smeared his blistered back with aloe vera cream.

''This should help,'' she told him as she sat astride his towel-draped hips. ''I thought you said you never burn.''

''I don't. I haven't had a sunburn since I was a little kid.''

''Know what?'' she asked brightly.

''I have one now,'' he mumbled.

She laughed.

''It's not funny.''

Composing herself, she tried to be sympathetic. ''I'm sorry. I know it must hurt. Let me get your legs.'' As she applied the balm to the back of his legs, she was especially careful of the injured area on his calf. ''When do your stitches come out?''

''They're due out tomorrow, but Kyle said it could wait until we get back.''

An idea struck Eve, and she asked, ''Are you still taking medication?''

He nodded. ''Twice a day. Kyle said that I need to take it for a week or so.''

''That may be your problem. Where's the bottle?''

''In my shaving kit.''

Just as Eve suspected, the medication had a sticker warning that it caused sun sensitivity. ''Always read the labels, sir.''

''Yes, ma'am. Would you put some more lotion on my shoulders. Oh. Yes. Right there. Ahhh. You have the hands of an angel. I would marry you for that if nothing else.''

Eve swatted his butt playfully, then stroked lotion on his arms.

Such fine arms they were. Strong, well muscled. Perfect to hold her with.

And his back was magnificent. Broad, solid. Sexy.

She bent to kiss a small, flat mole on his shoulder blade. ''Turn over,'' she murmured against his hot skin, ''and I'll do your front.''

As he turned over, the towel shifted, and he was momentarily exposed. He was definitely and magnificently aroused. He looked sheepish, then grinned. ''What can I say? I stay that way around you. At least it didn't get sunburned.''

She tried to act shocked, but he was so darned appealing with his boyish outrageousness, that she found herself laughing again. ''No, and it seems to be working fine.''

As she poured a dollop of aloe into her palm, he unhooked the bra of the blue bikini suit she still wore. ''What are you doing?'' she squealed.

''Getting rid of this,'' he said, tossing the top aside. ''I want to look at you. And touch you.'' He held out his hand for lotion, and she poured a bit into his palm.

As she stroked his reddened chest, he stroked hers. He made long, sensuous sweeps over her torso, then upward to cup her breasts. ''Beautiful,'' he murmured. ''Lean closer. Let me taste.''

A thrill ripped through her, and her breasts swelled in his hands as she leaned forward. He moved one nipple to his mouth, and his tongue made a slow circle around the hardened tip before his lips closed around it. "Ummm. Delicious."

Her hands stilled. She forgot to stroke his fevered skin. She didn't move lest the feeling escape; she completely lost herself in the heavenly sensation of his mouth as he pulled at her breast.

His sucking seemed to stimulate nerves that ran from breast to womb and set her throbbing with a bittersweet ache. He blew against the wetness he'd left, then moved to the other breast to lave. The sensation increased tenfold until she squirmed against him.

He slid his fingers into the bottom of her suit, then slipped inside her body. She threw her head back and drew air between her clenched teeth.

"Like that?" he asked.

"I love it."

"Why don't you take this off?" He tugged at the skimpy fabric.

"But your sunburn—"

"We can be very careful. I'll let you do all the work."

As she moved away to take off the rest of her bathing suit, he reached into the bedside table for protection. He winced.

"Here," she said. "Let me."

She stripped the condom from the package and with his hands guiding hers, she rolled it over his hardness. It was a marvelously erotic experience. She found that she wasn't at all shy with Matt. He made her feel like the sex goddess of the universe, and she reveled in the feeling.

He praised her body and stroked her in the most intimate of ways, and she blossomed in his hands.

When he drew her breast to his mouth again, she arched her back and rubbed her nipple across his lips, then pressed herself hard against his mouth.

She grew hotter and hotter until the ache for him was unbearable. "I want you, Matt. I want you."

"You've got me, darlin'." He raised her hips and eased her onto his tumescence.

She almost screamed as he filled her, deep and hard. She needed no instruction with this new experience; instinct took charge, and she rode him in a dogged quest for fulfillment, knowing that the better each thrust and grind felt to her, the closer she was to the finish she sought.

"Yes," he murmured. "Yes, darlin'. That's the way. That's the way."

Her climax erupted in a gloriously violent series of sensations. She sat astride him, head thrown back and trembling as the aftershocks rolled over her. She felt him throb inside her, and her sensitivity was intensified. He stroked her breasts and rubbed her belly, and the contractions seemed to ripple on and on.

Tears rolled down her cheeks, and she bent to rest her forehead on the pillow beside his ear. "Oh, Matt, what am I to do? I love you so."

"Do?" He chuckled. "Why, sugar, just keep on lovin' me. Those are the sweetest words I've ever heard. They're worth more than anything to me. I'd endure a sunburn every day if that was what prompted this."

She sat up quickly. "Oh dear, your sunburn. Did I hurt you?"

"Nope. But it's beginning to sting a little now. I think a little more lotion might help." He gave her a devilish grin.

The next morning, Eve was very quiet on the drive back to Hobby Airport in Houston. She was very quiet on the flight to San Antonio. Matt seemed concerned about her withdrawal and had asked about her mood several times. She couldn't explain. How could she explain to him that she was terrified of being in love with someone like him?

Terrified that he was going to break her heart?

Matt was—well, Matt was perfect. He was handsome, bright, enormously successful, a wonderful person, fun to be with. Perfect.

And despite the things Matt said, she was just plain Eve Ellison. Too tall. Awkward. Unsophisticated. She had a dilapidated old farmhouse and a ragtag bunch of rejected animals. She didn't travel in the fast lane or hobnob with the country club set. She was more comfortable in blue jeans and old sneakers than designer dresses and high heels. What could he see in someone like her? Irish was the beauty of the family. Irish had the charm and savoir faire.

Oh, sure, Eve was bright enough, and darned good at her job, but men like Matt didn't fall in love with women because they were good at their jobs.

Was Matt really in love with her?

Why?

She'd asked him that the night before. He'd only

laughed, kissed her nose and said, "Because you're so darned loveable."

That was no answer. She sighed.

"Honey, please tell me what's wrong," he said as they drove another rented car from the San Antonio airport.

"Do you really love me?" she asked.

"I really do. I'm head over heels crazy in love with you. Honey, I've proposed about a dozen times. And I've never proposed to another woman in my entire life."

"Never?"

"Never. Unless you count Mary Jane Beavers. But we were in the second grade at the time. She agreed to marry me, but her family moved to Wisconsin two weeks later."

Eve laughed. "You nut."

"Ah, good. You laughed. Does that mean that the funk has lifted?"

"I didn't mean to be a wet blanket, it's just that I'm troubled. People don't fall in love so quickly, Matt. Relationships take time."

"Not always. I knew when I saw you walking down the aisle at Irish and Kyle's wedding that you were the woman for me. I knew it instantly. I proposed to you then, didn't I?"

"But you were joking. You didn't even know me. And what in the world would somebody like you want with somebody like me?"

"Honey, you have a serious image problem that we need to work on. And I plan to show you how special you are."

Twelve

"It's eerie in here, isn't it?" Eve asked as she stood beside Matt in the famous stone mission.

"Very. And even if they've seen the John Wayne movie, people always expect the Alamo to be bigger."

"There's such tragedy here." She was surprised to discover tears stinging her eyes. She blinked them back and squeezed Matt's hand. "Fighting is such a waste."

He brought her fingers to his lips. "Travis, the commander, was supposed to be a jerk, but thinking of Davy Crockett being killed here has always bothered me. Maybe it was because I always thought of him as Fess Parker."

"Did you watch those old TV shows, too?"

"Yep. When I was about six or seven. Jackson

and I also insisted on having coonskin caps just like Davy's, and we went out bear hunting a time or two. Thank God we never found one. 'Course Highland Park was never known for an abundance of bears.''

With Eve chuckling at the notion of the two boys bear hunting in the ritziest section of Dallas, they walked outside into the plaza. Bright afternoon sunlight filtered through the huge oaks on the grounds that were now surrounded by downtown San Antonio.

''Want to go to Fiesta Texas?'' he asked. ''They have some roller coasters you might want to try. One of them goes backwards.''

''Backwards? Wow.'' As they crossed the street on the way back to their riverside hotel, Eve said, ''I'd love to go, but how is your sunburn today? You don't need to aggravate it.''

''It seems to be okay. And that sunblock you smeared on me must have a PF of 200. It feels like lard. I don't think I'll blister, but I might fry.''

She laughed and pulled him along to a little shop that displayed beautiful stained glass in the window.

As they stood admiring the craftwork, Eve felt something furry brush her bare ankles and heard a soft, plaintive mewling. She looked down to find a tiny kitten, its white-and-black fur grimy and matted, crying at her feet.

''Oh, precious,'' she cooed, scooping up the poor, pitiful thing. ''Oh, Matt, look. He's no more than skin and bones. He must be lost.''

''Or abandoned.''

''Surely nobody would toss out such a darling kitten. With the black mask on one side of his face, he reminds me of the Phantom of the Opera. Let's ask the merchants around here. Maybe one of them knows where he belongs."

None did.

When they had tried every shop for two blocks each way without any luck, they gave up the search.

"Matt, we can't just leave the poor baby on the street. He's hungry. And frightened."

"Maybe we can take him to the SPCA."

Horrified by the notion, she glared at him. "Bite your tongue, mister!"

"Sorry, honey."

"I'll find him a good home. But first we need to feed him, then take him to the vet. He probably has worms."

"*Worms?* My God, Eve, put him down."

"Oh, good grief, Matt. Don't be such a sissy. Go find the poor baby something to eat, and I'll sit down on this bench and wait for you."

Her wish was his command, so he went in search of food. He didn't have any idea what to feed a kitten except milk. The waiter at a nearby Mexican restaurant didn't want to let him have a bowl, but Matt paid him twenty bucks and walked out with a plastic bowl, a carton of milk and a pocketful of cellophane-wrapped crackers.

"Will this do?" he asked Eve when he returned. "I didn't think he'd like tortilla chips and salsa."

She looked at him oddly. "We'll see. Crumble some crackers in the bowl and pour in a little of the milk."

Matt set the bowl on the bench and followed her directions. The kitten started wiggling as the milk splashed into the bowl, and when Eve put the kitten next to it, the little fellow began devouring the con- coction in a hurry.

"I think he likes it," she said, flashing Matt a million-watt smile. "You did good."

Matt nearly popped his buttons. "I did, didn't I?"

She laughed. "While our little buddy is finishing his lunch, perhaps you could find a box to put him in so that we can take him to the vet."

"No problem."

Matt did better than that. He found a super-size drugstore on the next block that had a small pet car- rier. He bought the carrier, some kitty treats, a little ball and a cloth mouse that squeaked. The whole bill was less than the bowl and the milk.

The vet's bill was considerably more.

But Matt paid it gladly. He would have built the young animal doctor a new clinic just to keep the blissful smile on Eve's face.

"Isn't he precious?" she said as she took the freshly bathed, dipped and medicated kitten from the assistant and cuddled him against her cheek.

"He's a fine-looking fellow, all right." And Matt had to admit that he was a cute little guy now that he was cleaned up.

"I think Phantom would be a good name for him," she said as they drove back to the hotel. "Don't you?"

"Sounds good to me."

"Do you think the hotel will mind if we keep him in the suite with us?"

"Naw. We'll sneak him in in a Neiman Marcus sack."

Eve giggled. "I'm game."

They had to settle for a giant shopping bag that the carrier would fit into, but they had an adventure running around, making preparations for their clandestine operation, and snickering like two kids planning to smoke behind the garage as they poked a few pencil holes in the sack for air.

When they finally walked into the lobby with Matt carrying the huge sack with the kitten and carrier and Eve carrying a smaller sack with a litter box and litter, they didn't dare look at each other or they would break up. They hurried to the elevators and got on an empty car. Unfortunately, a middle-aged couple and a pinch-faced teenage girl rushed through the doors just as they were beginning to close.

Phantom mewed from the depths of the sack.

Matt cleared his throat loudly, shifted the sack, and studied the elevator buttons. Beside him, Eve hummed "The Music of the Night" and kept her eyes on the ceiling.

Phantom mewed again.

The middle-aged woman, who looked as if she'd eaten a few too many prunes for breakfast, turned sharply and glared at Matt. "Is that a *cat?*"

"Certainly not," Matt replied.

Phantom mewed again.

The woman glared. "That *is* a cat in that bag. And this hotel doesn't allow animals."

The teenage girl rolled her eyes and hunched her shoulders as if she wanted to seep through the cracks. Her father studied his fingernails.

"Madam," Matt said, tipping his cowboy hat. "Rest assured that this is not a cat. I'm carrying our baby in here."

The woman gasped; the teenager strangled on a giggle; the man rose up on his toes.

Thank heavens the elevator stopped just then and the trio rushed off because Eve could barely contain her laughter until the doors closed. Then she howled.

"Our *baby?*" she choked out between gales of laughter. "Did you see that poor woman's face? I thought she was going to explode."

They were still laughing when they reached the door to their suite. Once inside, Matt caught her to him and rocked her from side to side. "I can't remember when I've laughed so much. I feel as crazy as a kid."

"Me too." She suddenly pushed away. "We forgot poor Phantom! Let's get him out, and see if he's okay."

The kitten was fine, just irritated with being shut up. Once he was out, he ran around the room chasing the little ball Matt tossed to him. Matt and Eve stood arm in arm, smiling and watching the little fellow play.

"I'm afraid we missed our afternoon at Fiesta Texas," Matt said. "Want to go tonight?"

She shook her head. "I'm a little tired. Why don't we order room service and watch a movie here."

"Sounds good to me."

Matt had a steak, a baked potato and a big salad; Eve had the same but without the steak. Phantom dined on filet of sole, then curled up on Matt's lap while they watched an old movie on TV.

When a knock came at the door, Eve untucked her legs from the couch and said, "That must be room service to collect the dishes. You and Phantom stay put, I'll get it." She padded barefoot to the door and opened it.

The man standing there with a bottle of wine wasn't a room service waiter.

He smiled. "Good evening. I'm Ron Futch, the assistant hotel manager."

Eve's heart almost stopped. The jig was up. The elevator people had complained about the cat, and the manager was here to throw them out. How humiliating. "I—I can explain everything."

"Honey, what's up?" Matt said from behind her.

She whirled and tried to motion him away with subtle gestures and exaggerated facial expressions. He didn't get it. Instead he ambled toward the door in his socks and with Phantom cradled in the crook of his arm.

"Honey?"

"It's Mr. Futch, the hotel *man-a-ger,* dear." She continued to motion him back.

"Hey, Ron," Matt said coming to the door. "How's it going?" The kitten was crawling up his shirtfront when Matt stuck out his hand to the man.

"Great, Matt. It's good to see you. You caught Harve out of town, and I just got a breather. Glad to have you staying with us. Thought you might enjoy this." He held out a bottle of champagne. Very expensive champagne. "Shall I ice it down for you now?"

"No, I'll do it later. Thanks. Ron, this lovely lady

is Eve Ellison." He plucked the kitten from his shoulder. "And this fellow is Phantom."

The manager smiled and nodded. "Miss Ellison." He scratched the kitten's head. "Cute little thing. Anything you or Miss Ellison or Phantom needs?"

"No. Everything is fine. Thanks."

Futch said his goodbyes and left. The moment the door closed, Eve slumped against it and let out a big sigh. "I can't believe he was delivering champagne. I nearly had a stroke when he said he was the assistant manager. I thought he was going to toss us out on our ear."

"Not likely," Matt said. A slow grin slid over his face. "My folks own the joint."

When the implication of what he said dawned on her, Eve's eyes narrowed. "Your folks own— Why, you *rat!*" She plucked an embroidered pillow from a nearby chair and whopped him on the head. "You dirty rat!"

Laughing and shielding his head, he moved away, darting and dodging to avoid her licks. She followed him, hitting him every chance she got.

Soon they were running around the suite laughing as she continued to wield the soft weapon. Finally they both fell onto the couch, and she clutched the pillow to her chest. "I can't believe you tricked me like that. I feel like a total idiot."

"It was only a joke. I thought we had fun sneaking Phantom in. Didn't we?"

"I guess so. But I don't like to be the butt of jokes, Matt. I never have. I suppose it comes from some extremely hurtful things that happened when I was a kid, but I really don't like being duped. In fact, I hate it. Irish says that I'm overly sensitive, and perhaps so, but nobody enjoys being made a fool of or being a laughingstock.''

Matt put the kitten on the floor and took Eve into his arms. ''Oh, honey. I'm sorry. I wouldn't hurt you for the world. I'm a first-class jackass. Will you forgive me?''

She was silent for a moment, then sighed. ''Yes, of course. But please don't do it again.''

''I won't. I swear.''

''Fair enough.'' Snuggling into the warm circle of his arms, she asked, ''Do your parents really own this hotel?''

''They really do. They live here now.''

''Here? In the hotel?''

''Yep. One floor up. They built the hotel and moved here from Dallas about eight years ago.''

''I think I remember them from Irish's wedding. Aren't you going to visit them while we're here?''

''Nope. They're on an Alaskan cruise. They won't be back until the end of next week, but when they return, I would like for you to get to know my parents. I think you'll enjoy them. They're good people. My mother has a cat. A fourteen-year-old ball of fluff named Abigail.''

''Then I know I'll like her.'' She snuggled closer.

''Want some champagne?''

''The bubbles tickle my nose and make me sneeze.''

''Then I'll wipe your nose.'' He kissed the tip and went to ice the wine.

A rough tongue licked Matt's chin, and he opened one eye. Phantom stood on his chest. In fact, Phantom had spent most of the night on his chest...when Matt wasn't otherwise occupied.

Phantom mewed.

Matt moved the kitten and turned over on his side.

Fur tickled his cheek and the small grainy tongue licked the tip of his nose.

Matt opened his eyes a slit, and a pair of baby blues stared at him. Phantom mewed again.

"Shhh," he warned the cat, glancing to Eve's sleeping form.

Eve lifted her head. "What time is it?" she mumbled.

"Breakfast time for cats, I guess. Let me go see if I can find something in the refrigerator to keep him quiet. Do you think cats like peanuts or champagne?"

"No, they like cat food. I saved the rest of his fish from last night. Try that." She covered her head with a pillow.

Matt dropped a kiss on her shoulder and got up with the kitten.

Phantom turned up his nose at the leftover sole.

"For somebody who was hungry and homeless only yesterday, you sure have gotten picky, my friend."

The tiny cat mewed and entreated with big blue eyes the same color as Eve's. Matt's heart melted. They tried several packages of goodies from the refrigerator until Phantom settled on pâté.

"I'll say this for you, buddy, you've got a refined palate."

Matt heard the shower going and decided to join

Eve. They were due at the airport in a couple of hours, and he didn't want to waste a minute of private time with his lady.

Matt and Eve missed their flight to Austin, but they caught the next plane.

"Drink fast, folks," Marci, the flight attendant told them as she passed out juice. "It's only thirty minutes from takeoff to landing and we're ten minutes gone already."

"I think you're going to like Austin," Matt said. "It's one of my favorite places in Texas. It has a different sort of atmosphere than anywhere else in the state. Very laid-back and mellow, but very alive at the same time."

"Didn't you go to the university here?"

"Yep. My junior and senior years. And I got my law degree at the University of Texas."

"I keep forgetting that you're an attorney. Why aren't you practicing law?"

"Guess you could say I got sidetracked trying to double my million."

She frowned. "I don't understand."

"Well," he said, stopping to take the last pull from his orange juice. "It's something that Grandpa Pete thought up. All the family money started with him, you know. They struck oil on his property years ago, and he made a fortune. The wells are still pumping. Plus, he invested his money in all the right places. He owns big hunks of blue chips and banks and real estate.

"The deal was that Grandpa Pete paid for the educations of all his grandchildren, anywhere they wanted to go to school, and for as long as they wanted to continue. When each of the five of us graduated, he gave us a million dollars and five years to double the million. If we did it, he gave us another ten million."

Eve's eyes widened. "*Ten*—? Ten million dollars? To each grandchild? I knew he was wealthy, but— *Pete?*"

"Yep. That loveable old coot in the long braids and overalls is loaded. He gave each of us an education plus eleven million dollars, plus who knows how much to his daughters, my mother and my aunt, and he still has more than all of us put together."

"So you all doubled your money?"

"Yep. Every one of us. I started Crow Airlines twelve years ago. I sank every penny I had and all that I could borrow into buying a small company that had gone bankrupt. I sweated a few bullets that first five years, but I made it."

"You worked very hard, didn't you?"

He nodded. "We all did. We all doubled our money by working hard or working smart." He chuckled. "Everybody except Jackson, that lucky son of a gun."

"Buckle up, buckaroos," the attendant said. "We're coming into Austin, home of bats and long-horns and the hottest chili in the state. Yee-ha!"

Thirteen

Careful to slather on sunscreen, Eve and Matt put on shorts, fitted Phantom into a baby sling that Matt found, and spent the day at a wonderful festival on the grounds of one of the art museums. They visited every booth, ate roasted corn on a stick, watched jugglers and mimes, and listened to roving mariachi players.

Eve bought a small watercolor and several beautifully carved, gaily painted wooden flowers on long curving stems. Matt bought a bronze bear, considerably more expensive than her finds, for Jackson's upcoming birthday, and a hand-braided belt for himself.

"Oh, I love Austin," she said as they walked back to the car with their purchases. "The limestone hills are so pretty and the people are neat."

"I like Austin, too. It's my favorite town in Texas."

"Then why don't you live here?"

He shrugged. "Business reasons, I suppose. Crow headquarters is in Dallas. But I come here every chance I get. Jackson loves the place, too. We used to spend a lot of time on Sixth Street."

"What's Sixth Street?"

"Mostly bars and clubs. That will have to wait until next trip. Unless you want to stay over an extra night—which is okay by me."

"It would be great fun, but I have the animals at home to think about. Jimmy is being a sweetheart to care for them while I'm gone, but I need to get back. I have butter to churn and a million other things I need to do at home before Monday morning. And next week is going to be very busy. I have lots of ideas for a new Crow campaign. I hope you'll be pleased with what we come up with."

"I can't imagine not being pleased. Everything you do pleases me." He helped her into the car, then leaned inside and kissed her. "Everything."

Late on Saturday afternoon, Matt dropped off Eve and Phantom at her vehicle in the parking garage near her office. He stowed her bags in the backseat and strapped in the carrier with the kitten inside.

He took Eve in his arms again. "I'll be happy to follow you home and help with the chores."

She shook her head. "Thanks, but you're too big a distraction. Besides, I know that you have work to catch up on as well. Remember, I eavesdropped on all those calls you got on your cell phone, and I saw

the size of your message stacks. Call me tomorrow
if you have time."

"I'll make time." He kissed her again. "These
past few days have been terrific for me. And for you
too, I think. I love you so much, Eve."

"And I—I love you, Matt."

A car stopped beside them. "Hep you folks?"

A private security guard was grinning at them.

"Nope, pardner," Matt told him. "I can handle
this all by myself."

Eve laughed and got behind the wheel.

Matt waited until she pulled away to fall in after
her.

Already he missed her.

The following week at the agency was a frenzy of
activity. Eve had come back from the trip brimming
with new confidence and abundant happiness as well
as a mountain of information and ideas that needed
integrating into a hot new campaign for Crow Airlines. She hired another writer and another art director and had countless meetings with her team brain-
storming concepts for the new campaign.

Matt, too, was busy catching up, but the two of
them had dinner several times, once with Kyle and
Irish, and they talked on the phone at least twice
every day.

Being in love was absolutely glorious. Her step
seemed lighter, her mind sharper. The world was
lovely. And if there were problems with Matt's being
a client of the agency, they could work it out. She
was confident of it.

When the weekend approached, he asked, "Want

to fly to El Paso or to Corpus Christi? We didn't have time to go either place on our last trip. Or how about the valley? I could show you my cousin's orange groves, and we could go over to Mexico and do some shopping.''

"I have a better idea. Why don't we send some of the others on the team? They need to get a feel for the airline and the fun places to visit, and I need some help repairing my back porch. How are you at repairing porches?"

"Fantastic.''

Saturday morning as Eve was putting the last of the butter from the churn into the press, Matt arrived with a carpenter's truck following his sports car.

When Eve tried to protest, he said, "Honey, Russell is great with porches, and hiring him is cheaper than paying another hospital bill, plus it'll give us time for other things. How's Phantom? Is Charlie still giving the little guy grief?"

"I'm afraid so. But Ailda, Sam Marcus's fiancée, has agreed to take Phantom. They're going out of town this weekend, so I'll be dropping him off Monday morning on my way to work."

"I'll miss him."

She sighed. "Me too, but I can't keep them all. Ailda is very nice. She'll take care of him. Say, if Russell is going to do the porch, you can help me plant some flowers by the gate. I've been wanting to set out some butterfly bushes ever since we saw all those glorious creatures in Galveston. And roses. I'd love to have some roses."

They decided to deliver Pete's butter personally,

then stop in Tyler to buy plants. Matt assured her that Tyler was the rose capital of Texas and had every variety known to man—at least, the ones that did well in Texas.

Matt drove her vehicle so they would have room for the plants they planned to buy on the way home. The drive to Pete's place took almost two hours, but it was well worth the drive. It was beautiful country, with tall pines and various oaks and other kinds of trees scattered through the great green thickets. No wonder her folks were anxious to move to the area.

Pete was delighted with their visit, and Gomez ran to Eve and began licking her hand. She knelt and hugged him and he wiggled and wagged with excitement. "Have you been a good boy with Pete?"

"He's a fine dog," Pete said. "We rub along together pretty good. He's been a lot of company."

When Gomez seemed to have his fill of her attention, he went back to Pete's side, sat down, and looked up at the old man with bright eyes and lolling tongue. Pete smiled and patted his head.

"Gomez seems to be very fond of you," she said. "Would you like to keep him for a while? Maybe permanently?"

Both man and dog seemed pleased with the new arrangement. Gomez had always needed individual attention and a firm hand; Pete was the perfect master for him.

"We brought you some more butter," Eve said. "I made two pounds this morning."

"Oh, boy," Pete said. "I surely did enjoy that last batch you sent. Ate a pound of it this week, mostly with biscuits and ribbon cane syrup. Mighty good, mighty good. Sold the other two pounds. I'll get your money."

"No, no," Eve said. "The butter is a gift for all your help."

Pete and Matt showed Eve around the trading post with its strange assortment of goods and the "museum" which consisted mostly of a few arrowheads and a live rattlesnake. She met Alma Jane, who was frying chicken in anticipation of the lunch crowd. It amazed Eve that a man of Pete's wealth chose to run a general store in the country, but she supposed that he enjoyed it.

She was fascinated with the huge Indians and bears and cowboys that Pete had sculpted from logs with a chain saw. She was especially captivated with a large eagle that he'd just finished.

"You actually carved this with a chain saw?" she said, running her hand over the rough-hewn image.

"Yep. Oh, I do a little finish work here and there with a wood chisel and sandpaper, but I do most of it with a chain saw. Kyle's right good at it, too. Matt here never did take to it much."

They went upstairs to see Pete's extensive library and stayed for lunch. Afterward, they said their good-byes and drove to Tyler.

At the nursery where they stopped, Eve bought six rose bushes, two butterfly plants and a flat of yellow marigolds. Before evening, Matt helped her plant all of them.

"It's beginning to look a lot better around here," she told Matt when they stopped for a glass of iced tea. "I love the new roof, and when I get the place painted, it's going to look even better. What do you think—white with blue shutters to match the roof?''

''I think white with blue shutters is fine if that's what you want. Or maybe we could build a new house,'' he said.

''A new house?''

He nodded and wrapped his arms around her as they looked out over the pasture. ''After we're married.''

''Matt—''

''Okay, okay. I'll let it rest a while. How about we clean up and go boot scootin' at the Red Dog tonight? If you're gonna stay in Texas, you gotta learn to two-step.''

Fourteen

If Eve had been a fingernail biter, her nails would have been chewed down to the nub. Bart Coleman and Gene Walker, plus Nancy, Sam, Bryan and Eve sat in the conference room of Crow Airlines with Matt, his assistant, and three of his executives. The campaign that her team had put together after countless long days and nights of work was ready.

She thought it was choice; the team felt really good about it; Bart and Gene had been blown away when they'd seen the presentation the day before. But their opinions were worth nothing if the client didn't like their stuff.

Nancy stood at the head of the table conducting the last of the presentation—a dynamite set of slides showing a print blitz aimed at the family-oriented tourist. An up-tempo George Strait song provided background music.

When the last slide clicked into place, Eve counted to five to allow the full impact, then stood, turned up the lights, and turned on her brightest smile. "And that, ladies and gentlemen, shows that we have something new to Crow about at Crow Airlines."

Matt and the Crow people burst into applause. "Fantastic!" Matt said.

"Really impressive," a vice president said.

The others made equally complimentary remarks.

That feeling of dread that had kept her awake the night before melted away. Elation filled her; she felt like jumping onto the big conference table and belting out a Liza Minnelli song or doing a Rockettes number.

"Eve," Matt said, smiling broadly, "I think you and your group have come up with a winner. Bart, Gene, let's get together on Monday and work out the deal."

"Our office or yours?" Gene asked.

"How about 10:30 in my office," Matt said. "Will that work, Emily?"

His assistant nodded.

On that high note, the meeting broke up, and everyone began gathering their stuff. Eve winked at Nancy and Sam and tried to play it cool, but her excitement kept leaking out in a big grin. Everyone was grinning—except Bryan Belo. Spoilsport. She wanted to kick him.

Matt put his hand on her shoulder. "Great job, Eve. How about a drink and dinner to celebrate?"

Bryan shot her a smirk as he ambled from the room, but she was too happy to let it bother her. "You're on. I need to drop this material by the office first and tend to a few things there. Could I meet you somewhere later?''

"How about the Inn on Turtle Creek at six?" The Inn was a very special place indeed. Very exclusive, very intimate.

"I'll be there. I'll call Jimmy and ask him to take care of the animals."

The others from the agency had already gone, so Eve hurriedly packed her portfolio and left as well.

When she opened the front door at Coleman-Walker, someone tossed a handful of confetti and a cheer went up. The champagne corks were already popping, and Dexter whizzed by on his roller skates with a big tray of barbecued wings from the restaurant next door. "Great job," he yelled to her over his shoulder.

Everybody was laughing and whooping it up. Music blared from the intercom. More confetti was tossed, and Bart stood on a table and did an Elvis imitation as he sang "Jailhouse Rock" while Sam accompanied on a trash can drum.

The party was still in full swing when Eve left to meet Matt, and she was in a terrific mood. With a couple of glasses of wine under her belt, she decided to take a taxi. In fact, she'd arranged with Jimmy to take care of the animals in case she wasn't there the following morning. She just might stay at Matt's place.

"Congratulations again." Matt touched his glass to Eve's. "I can't get over what an excellent campaign you came up with."

She laughed. "You sound surprised. Didn't you think I knew my business?"

"No, no. Never that. I knew you were a talented lady, but it's so much better than anything we've ever had before, and I thought we'd had some great advertisements."

Smiling, she acknowledged his compliments and swirled the wine in her glass. Flickering candlelight turned the crystal to diamonds and the contents to glistening gold.

They had just finished a delicious meal in a quiet spot overlooking the patio with its lush greenery and muted lighting. Soft music played somewhere nearby. The sweet scent of freesia from a hanging basket tinged the air. Dear, sweet wonderful Matthew Crow was looking at her as if she was the most beautiful and desirable woman on earth.

She couldn't recall ever being so happy.

He reached across the table and took her hand. His thumb brushed lightly over her knuckles. "I love you, Eve. I love you so much."

"I love you, Matt."

"Truly?"

She nodded. "Truly."

"Will you marry me?"

She hesitated. Everything in her wanted to say yes. Still she hesitated.

"Eve, darlin', please say yes."

Such love shone from his eyes that she couldn't say anything else. "Yes," she whispered.

"Hot damn!"

She laughed.

"Let's get out of here. I want to kiss you properly."

He kissed her in the car; he kissed her in the garage; he kissed her in the elevator; he kissed her outside his door. And when they were inside, he did more than kiss her. He took her in his arms, swung her around, and let out a rebel yell that shook the rafters.

And he made slow sweet love to her with such poignancy that she wept with joy.

Life was good.

Something tickled Eve's nose. She wiggled it and brushed at the irritation. Something tickled it again. She wiggled her nose once more.

Matt chuckled, and she opened her eyes. He was lying on his stomach beside her, a black feather in his hand. "Wake up, sleepyhead. I have something to show you."

"What? A feather?" She sat up and fluffed the pillows behind her.

"No. Something better. I got so excited last night that I forgot to give you this. I've been carrying it around for weeks, hoping that I'd have the occasion to give it to you." He set a small velvet box on her tummy.

"What is it?"

"A ring." He opened the box to reveal a magnificent diamond solitaire. Alive with shimmering fire, it was large enough to be impressive, but not so large that it was ostentatious. "An engagement ring." He took it from the box and slipped it on her finger. "Like it?"

Tears sprang to her eyes. She couldn't help it. "I love it. Oh, Matt, you're serious." She threw her arms around him and wept.

"Darlin', of course I'm serious. Haven't I been telling you that since the first time I laid eyes on you?"

It took most of the weekend for it to sink in, but she finally realized that it wasn't a dream. Matthew Crow wanted to marry her. Her. Plain, gawky, too-tall Eve Ellison. No, not plain or gawky or too tall. She was exactly the right size for Matt. And she was beautiful and graceful. He said so.

They called Irish and her parents and told them the news, then spread the word in his family as well. All the relatives seemed very happy for them—especially Pete who declared that he was giving her that two million he had promised as a wedding present. She laughed and told him that he was off the hook; she didn't need a bribe to marry Matt.

Life was perfect.

Spirits were still high at the agency on Monday morning. While Bart and Gene were inking the deal, Eve met with her team to get the new campaign concepts rolling. Everybody was up and anxious to go—everybody that is, except Bryan Belo.

He was such a sourpuss.

Something had to be done about his attitude. She asked him to meet with her in her office.

When the door was closed behind him, she said,

"Bryan, I don't know what your problem is, but perhaps if you explain, we can work something out."

"I don't know what you're talking about."

"Of course you do. You're rude, surly, and deliberately disdainful of me and my position here. As far as I know, I haven't done anything to deserve your disrespect. What gives?"

She watched him struggle with what boiled beneath the surface. Anger? Hatred?

"What, Bryan? What have I done?"

"Done?" he shouted. "You haven't *done* a damned thing. Except sleep your way into a cushy job. Do you think you would have ever been made creative director over me unless you were screwing around with Matt Crow. Hell, no!"

Stunned, she could only stare at Bryan. "That's not true."

"Don't hand me that line of bull. Bart was ready to make me creative director until Crow waltzed in here and cut him a deal. 'Hire Eve Ellison and the account is yours,' he said."

"No," she whispered through dry lips, numb from the accusation. "That's not true."

"The hell it's not. I know for a fact that it is. Everybody knows it. Everybody knows you're sleeping with the client. Why else would a hot shop like this one hire a nobody from Ohio? Because she's got a rich sugar daddy, that's why. Ask Bart. Ask him." Bryan stormed through the door and slammed it behind him.

Eve dropped into her chair. She clasped her fingers together tightly, but she couldn't stop the shaking.

Bryan had lied to her. He was jealous of her position and he'd lied to hurt her. He was a vindictive, unhappy man who had lashed out because of his envy and anger. Matt would never do such an underhanded, manipulative thing that would make her the laughingstock of her colleagues.

Never.

He loved her.

She tried to breathe, but she couldn't. Her chest was paralyzed, and she couldn't get any air.

Eve was sure that she was going to die.

Fifteen

She couldn't fall apart now—not until she uncovered the truth of this thing. After a difficult struggle to get herself under control with long, even breaths and stern lectures, Eve grew composed enough to think. She had to handle this just right. Bryan, the worm, might be lying through his teeth just to make her miserable. She had to have the facts before she did anything rash.

Taking a deep, fortifying breath, she picked up the phone and rang the receptionist.

"Candy, is Bart back from his meeting yet? No? Would you please let me know the minute he returns? Thanks. And, Candy, hold all my calls. *All* of them."

Candy giggled and asked, "Even Matt Crow's?"

"Yes," she said quietly. "Even his. I'm 'in conference' to everyone except Bart."

She swung her chair around to stare out at the courtyard below.

The minutes seemed interminable.

She prayed.

She struggled with demons.

She waited. And planned.

A quarter hour.

A half hour.

Her stomach cramped. Her chest hurt. Her head was pounding.

The phone finally rang almost an hour later. "Bart and Gene are back," Candy said. "I told Bart you wanted to see him. Shall I ring his office for you?"

"No thanks, Candy. I'll just drop by in a minute."

"Nancy told me about your ring. She said it's a real rock. Congratulations, Eve. Matt's a terrific catch."

"Thank you," she said and hung up quickly.

She stood, brushed the wrinkles from her skirt and walked to the door of her office. She put her hand on the knob, straightened her shoulders, and pasted a smile on her face. "It's show time!"

A moment later, she knocked on the jamb of Bart's office door. "Busy?" she asked.

Bart looked up from a sheaf of papers and grinned. "Come on in."

"Did everything go well?"

"Slicker than goose you-know-what. Matt told me about your engagement. Congratulations—or do you say that to a woman? I forget the etiquette, but I'm tickled to death for you two."

"Thanks," she said, her cheeks beginning to quiver from the phony smile.

"Let me tell you again, Eve, what an absolutely first-rate job you've done with the account. You're a major asset to this shop."

Trying her darnedest to affect a casual, teasing tone, she chuckled and said, "You weren't quite sure of that when Matt twisted your arm to hire me, were you?"

Bart's smile died slowly, and something else in his expression made the rope holding her last hope begin to fray.

"Eve, I don't—"

"Oh, you don't have to be coy about it any more, Bart." She laughed gaily and winked. "I know about the deal Matt made with you."

"He told you? After the vows he made me swear, I'm surprised—"

Something in her expression must have betrayed her—and in truth she felt as if she'd just been laid open with a fillet knife—for Bart suddenly looked stricken.

"That bastard," she ground out despite her efforts to keep quiet.

Bart turned ashen and uttered a succinct profanity. "Oh, God, Eve." He rose slowly, his horror evident. "What have I done?"

She would not burst into tears. She would not.

"You've been truthful," she said very quietly. "Please accept my resignation effective immediately."

"Eve—"

"Please, Bart, don't say any more."

Her fingers squeezed tightly together, and the engagement ring bit into her flesh. She looked down at

the diamond, and its flash and fire seemed to mock
her. She pulled it from her finger and tossed it on
Bart's desk.

"Give that to your old fraternity brother the next
time you see him." She turned and walked briskly
from his office.

Eve stopped only long enough to empty her briefcase and portfolio of its agency-related contents and
grab her purse. She didn't say a word to Nancy or
Sam or Candy on her way out. She didn't dare.

Her hands clenching the wheel in a grip on her
emotions, she drove directly home.

Minerva and the dogs began dancing around her,
delighted to see her home in the middle of the day.
They followed her inside where she slammed and
locked the door. The phone began to ring.

She ignored it.

It kept ringing.

She yanked the plug from the wall.

Minerva and the dogs were joined by Charlie and
Pansy, and the entire group trailed behind her when
she stomped to her room and stripped off her smart
jacket and slacks and threw them on the floor.

"L'amour! L'amour! L'amour!" Caruso sang.

"Shut up!" she yelled at him as she yanked up a
pair of ratty sweatpants.

Surprisingly, she didn't hear another peep from the
living room as she pulled on a holey, paint-smeared
jersey.

Barefoot, Eve climbed into the middle of her bed
and gathered all her loyal friends around her. Only
then did she let go.

She took handfuls of Charlotte's fur and of Lucy's,

laid her forehead on the Saint's great shoulders, and wept from the depths of her shattered soul.

Charlotte howled, Lucy whined, Minerva grunted and Bowie growled as if an intruder were prowling about. Charlie nudged his way through the pack and bumped his head under her chin. Pansy licked her bare toes.

Still she wept. Never had she endured such pain, suffered such agonizing betrayal.

She cried buckets. She cried until her tear ducts dried up.

Finally, she got a package of chocolate chip cookies from the pantry, returned to bed with the animals, and ate the entire sackful. Every last crumb.

Then she started on a sack of macaroons.

Not only had Bart and Matt duped her, they had made her look like an ass in front of her colleagues. When she thought of how they must have been laughing behind her back, Eve wanted to curl up in a little ball and die.

Bowie's ears pricked up. Pansy hopped from the bed and went scurrying from the room.

A loud banging on her front door startled Eve.

"Three guesses who that is," she said to Minerva who began squealing and wiggling to get down. "Traitor," she called after the scurrying pig.

The banging grew louder, accompanied by yelling. She ignored the commotion.

"Fi-ga-ro, Fi-ga-ro, Fi-ga-ro!"

Bowie leapt from the bed and ran barking to the door. Charlotte deserted her, then Lucy. Only Charlie stuck by her.

Eve stroked him and laid her cheek on his head.

"He hurt me, Charlie. He broke my heart. I knew he would."

She continued to ignore the racket, and when Matt came to her bedroom window and began rapping on it, she calmly marched to the window and pulled down the shade.

She pulled down every shade and closed every drape.

After a while, Matt stopped knocking and banging and yelling, but when she peeked out a slit in the curtain, she saw that his car was still there. When she stuck her head out of her room, she saw him sitting on the front porch with his chair facing the leaded glass oval in the door.

Quickly, she pulled back.

"I saw you, Eve," he shouted. "You might as well let me in. I'm determined to sit right here until I talk to you."

"Go away!"

"Nope. I'll stay till Hell freezes over if I have to. You have to come out sometime."

"Ha! You'll starve to death before I come out."

"Not likely. I just ordered a pizza."

Furious that he was making her a prisoner in her own home—worse, in her room—she grabbed a beach towel and a roll of strapping tape and marched to the front door.

Matt smiled and stood.

His smile faded when he saw that she was covering the oval glass insert.

Six hours later, Matt was still sitting on the porch. An empty pizza box sat on the floor beside his chair, and he was sipping on a can of beer.

Determined that he wasn't going to catch her outside, she plugged the phone in long enough to call Jimmy and ask that he tend the outside animals.

Sleeping in a cramped car was the pits. And the damned mosquitoes nearly carried him away. The second evening, Jackson brought him a hamburger and a sleeping bag. And a cold six-pack. And mosquito repellent.

The brothers sat on the porch together, watched lightning bugs and drank beer.

"What in the hell did you do to make the woman so mad at you?" Jackson asked between pulls on his bottle.

Matt told him about the deal he'd had with Bart.

"That was a damned fool thing to do, little brother."

"I know that now, but it was the only thing I could think of to get her down here. She wouldn't answer my calls—"

Jackson chuckled. "She's not answering them now, either."

"Dammit, Jackson, it's not funny!"

"Sorry, but I've never seen you act like such an idiot over a woman. What's got into you?"

"Love, Jackson, pure and simple. I'm crazy in love with her. The minute I laid eyes on her, I knew that she was the one for me. Haven't you ever had that feeling about a woman?"

Jackson reared back in his chair. "Maybe. Once."

"What happened?"

"She wasn't interested." He shrugged.

"Anybody I know?"

"You met her. She was in Irish and Kyle's wedding."

"The psychologist?"

"Mmmm."

They watched the fireflies some more and drank another beer. An old bonding between them kept the silent companionship comfortable for several minutes.

"You ever think about her?" Matt asked.

"Yep. From time to time."

"Why don't you call her again?"

"I've been giving it some thought lately," Jackson said, rising and stretching. "How long you planning on staying here?"

"I don't know. Till I can talk to her, I guess, or until I can think of something better."

"You might try burning her out."

Matt could have sworn he heard a little gasp. His ears perked up, and he strained to listen. Nothing. The wind.

"I think I'll wait a while before I try fire or tear gas."

There. Again. Definitely a gasp. He grinned. He'd bet his last airplane that Eve was on the other side of the door listening to every word that had been said.

Matt stuck it out on the porch for two more days. He would have stayed longer, but he figured it wasn't getting him anywhere. He would try another approach.

He would call in the reserves.

Tipping his hat to the towel-draped front door, Matt climbed into his car and roared away.

* * *

Bart Coleman arrived that afternoon when she was painting the floral designs on the kitchen cabinets. When she saw who it was, she almost didn't let him in. But she sighed and relented. Bart had a lot to lose in this deal.

She invited him in and offered him coffee. He declined.

"Eve, I wouldn't blame you if you wanted to kick me in the knees over this mess, but I think that there are some things you ought to know. First, you're a damned good creative director, as good as any I've run across, and your work for the agency has been excellent. I'm not going to accept your resignation. I don't want to lose you."

"But, Bart, I can't—"

He waved off her protests. "With or without the Crow Airlines account, I want you to stay. You're fantastic. And you should know that the deal with Matt was only that you would be hired on probation. He understood that if you couldn't cut it, you'd be out, but he told me that you were terrific. Seems to me that he had more faith in your abilities than you did. The job is yours—on your own merits. Will you come back to work?"

His offer was tempting. Very tempting. She'd loved working at the agency. "Give me a few days. Let me think about it."

"Fair enough. And by the way, I fired Bryan Belo."

Flowers started arriving every hour on the hour. Roses. Dozens of them. All with the same card.

I love you. Talk to me.
Matt

He sent singing telegrams, jugglers, clowns, all with the same message.

Just as Irish pulled up to the gate, a helicopter flew over and dropped leaflets in her front yard. Hundreds of them.

Irish shaded her eyes and watched the pink papers flutter to the ground. "What in the world is that?" she asked.

Eve sighed. "Some more of Matt's handiwork, I imagine." She and Irish picked up several of the papers. They all had the same message.

"He's creative," Irish said. "I'll hand him that. When are you going to put the poor man out of his misery?"

"*His* misery? Sis, I'm the injured party here. He made a fool of me. I'll never forgive him for that."

Irish hooked her arm through Eve's. "Come, baby sister, I have some words of wisdom for you. Fix me a cup of herbal tea or something, and we'll discuss the ways of the world and of men."

A few minutes later, they were sitting at the kitchen table, and Eve had poured out her distress to Irish.

"He ought to be horsewhipped, no question about it," Irish said. "But there are a couple of things I need to know. First, despite everything that has happened, do you love Matt?"

Eve took a deep breath. "Yes."

"Do you think he loves you?"

She thought about all their time together, about all

the times he'd told her that he loved her. She thought about his words to Jackson that she'd overheard while he was camped out on her porch. "Yes, I believe he does."

"Then, sweetie, you're nuts to throw away the love of a wonderful man like Matt. There is pride, and there is foolish pride. Maybe he did some dumb things, and maybe you were hurt by them, but if you truly love each other, you can work things out. Believe me, Matt has learned his lesson over this. Honey, his heart was in the right place."

Eve swirled her tea around in the cup and watched the pink eddy. She looked up at Irish and smiled. "When did you get to be so wise?"

"A few months ago. I almost let something as silly come between Kyle and me. I felt exactly like you do. Promise me that you'll at least talk to Matt. Try to work this out."

"I'll call him."

Irish smiled and rose. "Do it now. I'm going home."

When they walked outside, they could hear a plane circling overhead. "Not more leaflets, I hope," Eve said, looking up.

About that time, a man jumped from the plane. In a few seconds, his parachute billowed open and he began drifting down toward the lane alongside the front gate.

Eve squinted against the sun, watching as the sky diver floated lower and lower. He came to a perfect landing not three feet from Irish's car. He pulled off his helmet, grinned, and bowed. "Afternoon, ladies."

"Matthew Crow!" Eve exclaimed. "You could have broken your neck."

He looked up from unbuckling his harness. "Would you care, darlin'?"

"Of course I would care."

He dropped his equipment, opened the gate, and walked to her. "Why?" he asked, lifting her chin so that she had to look at him.

"Because."

Irish cleared her throat. "I'll be leaving now."

"Because...why?" Matt persisted.

"Because I love you," she whispered.

He let out a whoop, swung her around, then planted a kiss on her that was the mother of all kisses. "Are you still going to marry me?"

"Maybe. As soon as we get a few things straight."

"Let's start right now." Laughing, Matt lifted her into his arms and strode into the house.

Minerva and the dogs followed behind, their rumps jerking with excitement. Pansy poked her head out from under the couch and Charlie raised his head and twitched his whiskers.

"L'amour! L'amour! L'amour! L'amour! L'amour! L'amour!"

"I couldn't put it better myself, my love," Matt said before he claimed her mouth in another kiss.

Epilogue

"Nervous?" Jackson asked Matt.

"How could you tell?"

Jackson grinned. "Because you've about worn a hole in the rug, and you've straightened that bow tie a dozen times. It's crooked again."

Matt yanked the bow loose and walked to the mirror in the pastor's study. "I never could tie one of these things worth a damn. And where in the hell is Kyle?"

"Kyle had an emergency, but he's on his way. Don't worry, he'll be here."

"I wasn't supposed to worry about Smith being here, but he didn't make it, either," Matt grumbled as he wrestled with his tie. "What's his excuse this time?"

"Grandpa said that he was in the hospital again. Broke something else."

"I think our cousin is accident prone, or he's lying to get out of wearing a tuxedo."

Jackson laughed. "You may be right. Smith never did cotton much to crowds or to sprucing up. Here, let me tie that thing before you ruin it."

While Jackson deftly looped the bow, Matt asked, "Did you ever give any more thought to calling your psychologist?"

"Olivia? Yes, I've given it a right smart of thought. I can't locate her."

"That's a shame. Can't Irish help?"

Jackson shook his head. "But I don't intend to give up. She's a special lady."

"If she's really special, Jackson, give it everything you've got."

"I plan to."

Kyle stuck his head in the door. "You boys about ready?"

"Where in the hell have you been, Kyle?"

"Performing my magic stitchery on a kid who had a run-in with a tree. I come bearing flowers." He grinned and handed Matt and Jackson rosebud boutonnieres.

"Nervous?" Irish asked Eve as she stood behind her and pinned the poofy headdress in place.

"A little," Eve said. "But not as much as I was afraid I'd be."

"You look gorgeous," Nancy Brazil said. "Radiant. And why shouldn't you? You're marrying a rich, handsome man who adores you, and you're going on a Mediterranean cruise for a month. I should be so lucky."

"You'll find that special fellow someday soon, Nance," Eve said.

Nancy snorted and picked up her bouquet. "Me? Not likely. I've given up on the idea of marriage. I don't need a man to make me happy. I'm going to start my own ad agency, work my butt off, and make my own fortune."

Eve and Nancy had become good friends, and she'd learned that Nancy's bravado often masked a tender, romantic heart. Eve and Irish smiled and winked at each other in the mirror. For the first time, Eve could see the family resemblance between them. She still wasn't the beauty that Irish was, but she was presentable.

No, darn it, Eve thought, she was attractive. Matt said so. Actually, he frequently said that she was beautiful, drop-dead gorgeous. The most stunning woman on earth. As lovely as any angel God ever created. And sexy as hell.

Maybe it was the Texas water or the sunshine, but sometime since she had arrived, an amazing transformation had occurred. Gone was gawky, plain Eve Ellison. When she looked in the mirror now, she saw an attractive, confident woman. She grinned. And one who was sexy as hell.

As Matt stood at the altar of the church in Dallas, gussied up in a tuxedo and his dress boots, he saw an angel walking down the aisle, an honest-to-God angel. He couldn't take his eyes off Eve as she came toward him on her father's arm. The only thing missing was a pair of wings.

She was celestial, a vision in white silk and lace

with the strings of real pearls he'd given her woven
through her lovely hair. When she looked at him with
those haunting blue angel eyes, his chest swelled and
his soul soared. He smiled.

This was his woman. His.

When Eve's gaze met Matt's, any apprehension
that still lingered vanished. She felt like an angel on
a cloud as she neared the altar. Joy filled her, and
she could feel its tingling warmth seep through her
pores and from her lips and her eyes until she was
sure that she glowed.

From the moment Matt took her hand until they
had said their vows, a sense of rightness settled in
her heart. She would love, honor and cherish him all
her days on earth—just as he would love, honor and
cherish her. This was her man. Hers.

When the priest told Matt to kiss the bride, he
planted a good one on her and held on to her so long
that the guests twittered. Eve didn't care. She held
on, too.

As they started down the aisle to exit the church,
Eve spotted Grandpa Pete in the second pew. He was
beaming. He winked and held up two fingers.

Eve laughed. She didn't need the two million that
Pete offered her to marry one of his grandsons. Love
made her the wealthiest woman in the world.

* * * * *

If you enjoyed what you just read,
then we've got an offer you can't resist!

Take 2 bestselling
love stories FREE!

Plus get a FREE surprise gift!

SILHOUETTE® Desire®

A hidden passion, a hidden child,
a hidden fortune.

Revel in the unfolding of these
powerful, passionate...

SECRETS!

A brand-new miniseries from
Silhouette Desire® author

Barbara McCauley

July 1999
BLACKHAWK'S SWEET REVENGE (SD #1230)
Lucas Blackhawk wanted revenge! And by marrying
Julianna Hadley, he would finally have it. Was exacting
revenge worth losing this new but true love?

August 1999
SECRET BABY SANTOS (SD #1236)
She had never meant to withhold the truth from Nick Santos,
but when Maggie Smith found herself alone and pregnant, she
had been unable to face the father of her child. Now Nick was
back—and determined to discover what secrets Maggie was
keeping....

September 1999
KILLIAN'S PASSION (SD #1242)
Killian Shawnessey had been on his own since childhood.
So when Cara Sinclair showed up in his life claiming he had
a family—and had inherited millions—Killian vowed to keep
his loner status. Would Cara be able to convince Killian that
his empty future could be filled by a shared love?

Secrets! available at your favorite retail outlet store.

Silhouette®

SDSRT

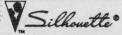

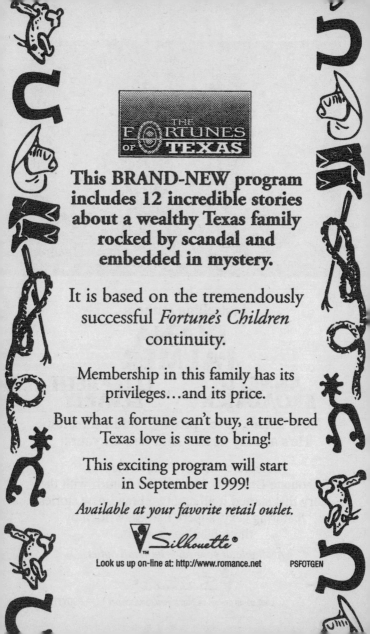